SIMPLE TRUTHS

RACHEL STOLTZFUS

Copyright © 2015 RACHEL STOLTZFUS

All rights reserved.

ISBN: 1523286563
ISBN-13: 978-1523286560

TABLE OF CONTENTS

ACKNOWLEDGMENTS	I
CHAPTER ONE	1
CHAPTER TWO	9
CHAPTER THREE	17
CHAPTER FOUR	25
CHAPTER FIVE	35
CHAPTER SIX	43
CHAPTER SEVEN	47
CHAPTER EIGHT	63
CHAPTER NINE	71
CHAPTER TEN	79
CHAPTER ELEVEN	91
CHAPTER TWELVE	95
CHAPTER THIRTEEN	115

CHAPTER FOURTEEN	121
CHAPTER FIFTEEN	129
EPILOGUE	139
NEIGHBORING FAITHS	143
ABOUT THE AUTHOR	151

ACKNOWLEDGMENTS

I have to thank God first and foremost for the gift of my life and the life of my family. I also have to thank my family for putting up with my crazy hours and how stressed out I can get as I approach a deadline. In addition, I must thank the ladies at Global Grafx Press for working with me to help make my books the best they can be. And last, I thank you, for taking the time to read this book. God Bless!

CHAPTER ONE

Rachel looked around her *mamm's* kitchen, shaking her head, and sighing at the mess of dishes, flour, spices, mixing and measuring spoons, and other evidence of her day of baking. She began scooping up and organizing the dishes, depositing spoons into bowls that had held batter, putting them all next to the sink. Wetting a washcloth, she wiped her work surfaces clean.

"My word, Rachel, it looks like the flour got into an argument with the milk and the spices!" Barbara Troyer quipped, smiling at her daughter.

"*Ya, mamm*, I just went straight from one recipe to the next. I'm paying for it now! Tomorrow, I'll clean in between pies, cakes and cookies." Rachel moved to wiping down the butcher-block table which had been baking-central since she started.

"How much did you get done? You have market in two days, you know." Her mother moved to the long table eyeing what

Rachel had made, finishing her inspection and smiling with satisfaction. "Good! You have had a productive day today."

"Yes, thank God. I want to earn enough that I can help you and *Daed* with bills and set aside enough for savings."

"Very good. You know it's not good to build up too much debt. The less you have, the better, when Thomas asks you to marry him," Barbara ran hot water into the sink squirting dish detergent into the water to make bubbles. She busied herself washing dishes, her back to her daughter.

"*Mamm*! We've only been courting for about a year. I'm still getting to know him. Besides... after what happened with his sister's beau, I'm still getting over that," Rachel's words slowed as she remembered that frightening time, absentmindedly shaking her hand over the trash can depositing spilled flour, spices, nut shells and fruit peelings.

Thomas Schrock's younger sister Mary had been courting with Jacob Yoder. Mary had always been restless, chafing under what she viewed as the restrictions of the Ordnung. She and Jacob had come up with what was initially a harebrained scheme to leave Hope Crossing, live among the *Englischers*, find work and maintain elements of their Plain lifestyle. Mary had urged Rachel to go away with them – Rachel, not wanting to leave her Amish community or lifestyle, refused. The two got into an argument and their long friendship fractured. Jacob, obsessed with the idea of living away from the Amish community, kept pressing Mary to change Rachel's mind.

When she didn't work fast enough, he told her they would simply force Rachel to leave with them. Mary, frightened, spoke to Thomas and their parents. Mr. and Mrs. Schrock spoke to Mr. and Mrs. Yoder, Jacob's parents. Jacob became enraged and went to Rachel's so he could kidnap her himself.

The two families, along with Rachel's mamm and daed, stopped him. Because of his plans to kidnap Rachel and his actual attempt, he was sent away from the district. Mary came to Rachel and apologized for her part in the situation. Rachel forgave her old friend, and they resumed their friendship.

"*Mamm*, I'm just grateful that I don't have to be fearful of Jacob Yoder. He's getting the help he needs, and maybe he'll choose to stay with the Englischers and be happy there. It's still sad that he had to be sent away with clear instructions never to come back. It must be so hard to be cast out of your home." Rachel picked up and dried a large mixing bowl.

"*Ya,* it is sad. But, remember Rachel, he chose his path in defiance of the *Ordnung* and the Lord's will. He needs help, but we can't give it to him here."

***

Two days later, Rachel stood behind her long table selling her baked goods to the *Englischers* and tourists who came to the northern Indiana community of Elkhart. In between customers, she counted how many baked goods she had remaining – only five. Next, she counted the money she had earned, zipping the vinyl pouch back up and stashing it between the boxes she used to transport her cookies, pies and cakes.

"So, how are you doing? It looks like you're about to run out, and we still have two hours before market closes today." Mary Schrock eyed what remained on Rachel's table. Mary had remained her best friend after that dark period of last year, and Rachel was glad for their continued closeness. There had been a change in her friend; she was quieter, less the wild child of the community and more contemplative, reserved and helpful. Yes, her self-centered, me-first attitude seemed to have been replaced with a more thoughtful, caring person.

This made Rachel happy; however, the spontaneous Mary had disappeared, too. That part Rachel missed; Mary was cautious now to a fault and worried about the strangest things, like would they have enough pies to make to the close of market. Clearly, if they ran out early, the world would not explode. The *Englischers* might be a little disappointed, but they would find other things to buy until next time.

"I am doing well today." Rachel smiled at her friend making the statement more to quell Mary's nervousness than anything else. "I still have one more cake and another box of cookies," She rustled around in the last box and took them out, setting them on the long table. She shifted them so they presented attractively. "How many do you have left?"

"I'm nearly out, too. I'm glad. I need to help *Mamm* and *Daed* with bills." Mary smiled as another *Englischer* approached.

"I'd like two dozen of those brownies, please." The *Englischer* was an older woman who had been to the market before, adding, "I have a meeting, and these will go over very well. Did you make them with walnuts?"

"*Ya,* I did. Does anyone at the meeting suffer from allergies to nuts?" asked Mary as she counted out 24 brownies and carefully deposited them into a box.

"No," the woman smiled and winked at her pulling out money to cover the purchase, "we just have several members who love nuts in their sweets."

"Great, *denki*! Enjoy them!" Smiling shyly, Mary gave the woman the box.

"Hello, miss! We would like... What kind of cake is that? Spice or peanut butter? And, oh, those chocolate chip cookies look absolutely delectable." A blonde woman walked up to the table waiting for the older woman to leave.

"This is a spice cake made with a cream cheese frosting." Rachel smiled at her two customers; one was a blonde, voluptuous woman with blue eyes, accompanied by a tall, well-built, yet slightly uncomfortable-looking gentleman with dark hair and what Rachel realized were beautiful green eyes. The woman stepped between them, commanding Rachel's attention; her bright green blouse and gray pants suit screamed of money and impropriety and her voice seemed vaguely antagonistic.

Rachel smiled again focusing her attention on the woman. She was still aware that the man was eyeing everything around him including her, from the Amish vendors in their prayer *kapps* and modest dresses to the handcrafted items and the baked goods that Rachel and Mary displayed on their tables.

"We'll take the cake and, oh, one dozen chocolate chip cookies." She seemed satisfied that Rachel was now totally attentive to her and not her partner. She pulled her wallet out of her large handbag and grinned in Rachel's direction, the rhinestones on the outer sides of the wallet flashing in the sunlight.

"Good," Rachel slid the cake into a small, deep box and placed another 12 cookies in a small box with a lid. "That will be thirteen dollars, please."

"Wow, what a bargain! We couldn't get away with this at a regular bakery." She laughed at her good fortune and Rachel thought that would be the end of it. "I have a quick question for you. How do you Amish people get along with no electricity or computers?" The woman continued to grin, her gaze expectant.

Rachel's mind stopped at the bluntness of the question. Opening and closing her mouth, she struggled for a reply that was both honest and polite. "Well, because we want to rely on God, we have chosen not to use electricity or other conveniences. We don't need electricity to get anything done."

The tall, black-haired man spoke up. "So, what do you use? Kerosene lamps? Come on, get real!" The woman shot a look of disbelief at Rachel. "You can stay close to God using a computer and electricity."

Rachel was used to these kinds of conversations which were mostly curious in nature, but the level of skepticism and mockery she was feeling left her quite uncomfortable. She was also thrown off a bit by the open, almost leering looks the man was giving her and the woman seemed overly effusive but not really friendly. She looked over at her partner then back at Rachel. His grin and looks were not missed by his girlfriend.

"I mean," the man leaned closer over the table, "a woman with your obvious charms and accoutrements would look incredible driving a sweet, sleek black Mustang with leather seats and all the bells and whistles." His girlfriend nudged him with her elbow none too gently.

"We want to practice humility and we believe that if we own possessions like computers, cell phones or cars, we become full of pride and risk moving away from God and his message." Rachel smiled in spite of her growing feelings of dislike at these two *Englischers*. She quickly slid the two boxes into a large bag.

"I give up!" The woman dropped a quarter on the table. "Here's a tip, and thanks for this. Y'all have a great day!" She turned on her heel, grabbing the black-haired man by the elbow and shoving him towards the parking lot.

"Well, that's that. A bit *glitzere* for my tastes." Rachel turned back to straighten her bags as though she might get ready to go home soon. Another hour and she would be completely out of things to sell for sure.

CHAPTER TWO

"I'm back." Once again the blonde woman with her dark-haired companion in tow stood in front of their table. Rachel smiled although she didn't really feel it inside. "Miss, my name's Melinda Abbott. This is my partner and boyfriend, Troy Scott. Here's my business card. I'm interested in talking more about the differences between the Amish and everyone else out in the world."

Rachel looked at the card reading the information on it. She saw Melinda's name, address and several phone numbers. At the bottom, she saw the woman's name, followed by ".com."

"What's this?" she asked, pointing to the last piece of information.

Troy, looking where Rachel was pointing, let out a hoot of disbelief.

"Lady, that's her website and email address! Are you for real?" he asked.

Rachel now felt much more than skepticism coming from the tall man – she felt outright disdain. Looking over at Mary, she saw that she had moved to stand right next to her.

"What's happening?" Mary asked as she took the card from Rachel.

"Apparently, you are the only two people on the planet that don't know what a website and email address is!" The woman laughed at the joke only she seemed to find funny.

"I am aware of what a website and email address is," Mary replied, her tone dripping with sarcasm. While Mary had come to be more modest and cautious, Rachel still saw the occasional "old" Mary, quick with the comeback and biting wit. In this situation, she didn't really fault her friend.

"Miss Abbott wants to meet with me to talk about the Amish," Rachel quickly put in. She knew that Mary's temper was still alive and well in Hope Crossing, although she prayed a lot more for tranquility and guidance these days. Rachel was also mindful that she needed to be cautious with these two.

"Hmmm. I'm glad you're interested in us, but we should meet only so we can explain to you why we believe and act as we do," Mary said. Following the new caution she had learned after the near-disaster with Jacob, she looked at Melinda with a new-found reserve in spite of her earlier quip. "Discussions are fine, but please understand we will only answer your questions." What Mary didn't say but heavily implied in her tone was that they would brook no mockery on the part of the

Englischers.

"Of course! Like I said, I am Melinda Abbott. And, you are..." Melinda extended a well-groomed hand in Rachel's direction, turning away from Mary.

"She is Rachel Troyer and I'm Mary Schrock," Mary reached around Rachel, shaking Melinda's hand lightly... very non-committal. Mary had gone on *rumspringa* and was very familiar with the ways of the English. She knew her friend Rachel had only left to attend one of the foremost baking and pastry making colleges in the Midwest. While at the Art Institute and Culinary School, Rachel had little time to go out and socialize like Mary did. As a result, she had not come into contact with the sleazy underbelly of the city. While these two were dressed well, they still carried the offensiveness of outsiders and sarcasm seemed to drip from every word the woman spoke. And, the man, well, she had met a number of men like him while she was out.

Troy wandered away from their table over to another table bearing a small baby quilt. "That's Troy Scott." Melinda pointed towards her partner as he browsed the tables that still had anything left on them. "Why don't we meet at that little cafe right outside Hope Crossing? It's called The 50's Cafe. Have you seen it?"

"*Ya,* we have. We can meet you the day after tomorrow. It will have to be home at the end of the day so we can finish our work," Rachel said.

"See *Ya* then! Thanks!" Melinda gave the two Amish friends a wide smile, then took Troy's hand and left the market.

Rachel looked at Mary and shrugged. "This should be an interesting conversation. I get the feeling they're only doing this for laughs, you know like 'look at the *dumm* Amish,' kind of thing."

"*Ya,* I know. We should have said no, but that would be un-Christian-like. We can just go and tell them about us, and they can accept it or not."

"Ya." Rachel busied herself packing up the last of her wares as did Mary. The two *Englischers* disturbed her peace of mind. She felt she would have to pray on what to say and the best way to put it so that they would understand. Hopefully, her first impression of them was wrong.

***

Outside, Troy unlocked a large, dark-gray Hummer, getting into the driver's seat. Melinda jumped up and into the passenger seat. Troy started out onto the road leading away from the market, easily navigating the roads that alternated between smooth dirt and black macadam.

"Man, Mel, I can't believe they honestly live like they say they do? How can they do all that baking and sewing with no electricity? By hand? Using kerosene lamps? Nah, they're pulling our legs!" Troy exclaimed.

"I think they do live like that, but I just can't get past their refusal to use computers, the Internet or electricity..."

"Hah! I couldn't believe it when that girl didn't know what your website was! I nearly started to laugh right in her face!" Troy said. Now he did laugh, guffawing loudly. By now, they were back on the state highway, driving at full speed back to their community.

"I like your idea of meeting with them. What'd you think of those funny little bonnets they wore? Did you get a load of those aprons and dresses they were wearing? Man, they looked just like something out of the 19th century," Troy said, giggling some more. What he and Melinda didn't know was that Rachel and Mary had just decided to tell Rachel's beau, Thomas, about their encounter.

"Mary, I want to invite Thomas to join us at that meeting. I was not getting a good feeling from that man, that Troy or whoever he is," Rachel said, packing her boxes together.

"*Nee*. I didn't, either. He was outright disrespectful and skeptical. Rude, even," Mary said, frowning. As she spoke, she loaded her own boxes and zipper bag of her day's earnings. The two young women carried their boxes out to their buggies, and then returned to help fold the tables and store them away for the next market day.

***

Melinda and Troy sat in their luxurious apartment, discussing Mary and Rachel, as well as their plans to capitalize on their encounter.

"Ya know, Troy... I think we can turn this into a huge public relations coup. This part of Indiana is, well, to call it 'behind the times' would be a kindness. These people are so close to modern technology, electricity, cars, computers, cell phones, smartphones, tablets, you name it... and they *refuse to use them*? How unreal is that? I mean, really!

"Hey, it sounds real good and all, their 'reasons' for refusing to allow them in their lives. I just can't accept that. 'Being closer to God and imitating his humility.' Get real!" Troy laughed, walking towards the kitchen.

"They could use a good nudge into modern times." Melinda took a bite of one of the chocolate chip cookies Rachel had made and sold to them. "Wow! I gotta say, for all their lack of modern supplies, they make a real mean chocolate chip cookie! This is absolutely to die for! Here, Troy, taste!" Melinda grabbed a second cookie jamming it into Troy's mouth. As he bit down, his eyes widened.

"No lie! This is better than any homemade cookie I've ever tasted!" Troy gobbled the cookie, and then returned to the business at hand. "You know, I'm thinking you could write up a P.R. piece. Send it to news outlets all over Indiana and the country. We want to modernize this part of the state, right? Your piece could do a lot to help us meet that goal. Those chicks *said* they don't rely on technology or modern conveniences, but I'll just betcha... Unleash them in a fully modernized kitchen and they'll change their minds. Just like that," he said, snapping his fingers.

"And about computers and cell phones? Once they learn how to browse the Internet, they'll be advertising their quilts, cookies and bookshelves. And, when they increase their earnings, you know who they'll be thanking? Us," Melinda giggled at the thought of Rachel and Mary surfing the net and finding porn. That would set their hats on fire for sure.

Troy snagged a second cookie and frowned, thinking of how he could help Melinda get that article written quickly. "You know, I can help you distribute that article, once you've written it. Melinda, they're backward. Like, way back in the early 1900's, backward. They have to be brought into the 21st century. If we bring them here, kicking and screaming, so be it. We're the ones to do it."

CHAPTER THREE

That evening, Thomas Schrock came to the Troyer home to visit Rachel. Sitting on the front porch, drinking fresh lemonade and eating some of Barbara Troyer's cookies, they swung back and forth on the hanging swing and talked.

"Mary told me about those two *Englischers* who bought from you today. She said the man was downright rude. What was your impression of them?" Thomas gave Rachel a look of worry; after her experience with Jacob Yoder the previous year, he didn't want to see her put in any more danger. These types of situations just made him realize how much he loved her and wanted to marry her.

"It was an... odd encounter. Mary is right. They wanted to discuss just why we refuse to use current technology. Troy was... dismissive at points and overly pushy at others... rude, even. He looked at me in a way that made me quite uncomfortable. The woman gave me a business card; she seemed more curious than anything, I think." Rachel fished the small card out of her apron pocket and gave it to him.

"Here, take a look. Melinda Abbott. Her address and several phone numbers. And this is her... her site web? Web site? Something! And some kind of address on the computer she uses," Rachel said, pointing to the website and email addresses printed on the front of the card.

Thomas read it carefully.

"They asked Mary and me to meet with them so that they could find out more about the Amish. We're going to meet them after supper the day after tomorrow," Rachel said. "At that 50's Cafe."

"If you do not mind, I would like to be at that meeting," Thomas held one end of the business card flipping the other end rapidly over his forefinger as he thought. *There is something odd about these people. Why do they want to know so much about us? We allow people to know something about us. That's inevitable. But we don't want the world to intrude on us and endanger our way of living and worshipping God. I doubt they want to respect us or our beliefs. Being there, I might be able to figure out their true intentions.*

"Thomas, *denki*! I think we need you to be there. I told you where the meeting will be held, and when. We need to know what you think," Rachel said, clasping her hands together so she wouldn't grab Thomas' hand. As she looked at him, she thought about how she had trusted Jacob Yoder before he had attempted to kidnap her.

"Okay, *denki*. I'll remember the day and time. Mary and I will pick you up after supper and we'll go in my buggy." Thomas tucked the business card away.

Mary was in her room in the Schrock house, thinking of Jacob and his plan to kidnap Rachel so that she, Mary, would have someone else to interact with and rely on. *What he tried to do to Rachel forced me to realize that the temptations of the world do affect us, even though we shield ourselves from them. Jacob's willingness to commit a crime was proof of that. Why am I thinking of this now?*

Mary came back to the present, bothered by her mind's persistence in going back to that frightening time. Walking slowly around her room, she realized that her earlier encounter with Melinda and Troy felt much like what she and Jacob had been thinking of as they made their plans to leave Hope Crossing.

Lord, I don't always see and understand what you know. Please give me your understanding of what happened today. Something about meeting these two people didn't feel... right, and I don't want anything to happen to my friends or anyone here in Hope Crossing.

As she finished praying, Mary yawned widely, realizing just how tired she truly was. She brushed her teeth and put her nightgown on. Unwrapping her hair from its bun, she ran a brush through her hair to remove the tangles. Before going to bed, she prayed once more.

"Mary, when we get ready to leave Hope Crossing, we're going to make Rachel leave with us, whether she wants to or not."

"But, Jacob, that would be wrong! I'm upset that she doesn't want to go, but I'm not going to force her to do what she doesn't want to."

"Mary, once we get to where we're going, she'll get over being mad. If she wants to continue living the Plain life, we can do that... How do you people get along without electricity or other conveniences?"

Mary suddenly jolted awake in her darkened room. *How had Jacob turned into that Melinda woman? And what did that mean?* Lighting her kerosene lamp, she pulled a writing pad and pencil from her nightstand, writing down everything she remembered from that disturbing dream. Setting the pad and pencil down, she wiped her forehead with shaky hands. Her brow wrinkled as she wondered just what the dream had meant. What was she supposed to figure out?

In the Troyer home, Rachel spent a similar night with disturbing dreams of Melinda Abbott and Troy Scott. Tossing and turning, when it was finally time for her to rise, she got out of bed slowly feeling as if she hadn't gotten a minute's sleep. Yawning, she shrugged on her dress, combed and braided her thick, long hair and coiled it into a neat bun. After setting her prayer *kapp* on her head, she slipped on her apron, tied it snugly around her waist and headed downstairs. Barbara Troyer looked up as Rachel dragged herself in, yawning and rubbing her eyes. Rachel was a morning person, so this was uncharacteristic for her.

"Daughter, you look as if you were awake all night long!"

"*Ya, Mamm*. I didn't sleep well last night. I may need some extra coffee to help me stay awake while I work today," Rachel stifled another huge yawn. "I had a really disturbing dream last night. Mary and I met some *Englischers* at yesterday's market, and they were more than curious about why we live the way we do. That's what my dreams were about – actually, more than dreams. They were nightmares... I can't say that they were mean, but they weren't really nice either. I felt so uncomfortable around them. Most times people ask about our lifestyle out of plain old inquisitiveness which is fine – natural to be curious. But, these two..."

"Daughter, God sent a message to you," Her father looked thoughtful as he sipped his hot coffee. "Your dreams are only disturbed like that when there is something amiss. Should I be at this meeting tomorrow night?" Abel Troyer was a strong man, a man of few words who tended to let the women handle their own issues. When he injected himself into a conversation, it was because he was worried, which Rachel could see reflected not only in his words but in the way his brow was furrowed and his lips pressed together.

Rachel thought for a few minutes and then shook her head. "*Nee*. Thomas will be there with Mary and me. If we learn what they are up to and we need you, I'll tell you right away. I promise, *Daed*."

"You only need to converse with these outsiders, and depend on Thomas. He has a level head on his shoulders and if they try something that is not right, he'll see it and put an end to things. You have a good man there, Rachel, but if anything happens and you need me, you know I will be there as fast as my buggy can carry me."

"I know, *Daed. Denki*." Rachel had always had a special place in her heart for her father. She knew he treated her special – spoiled her too much, her *mamm* had said from time to time – but his big heart and open arms and smile had always made her feel like she was on top of the world. He had taken the time to teach her little things when she was a little girl, always patient and kind, and he took extra care when Thomas had asked to court her. Their bond was always there, and last year he had come charging when she was in danger with Jacob.

***

The next night, Rachel answered the door to Thomas and Mary when they came to pick her up.

"*Mamm, Daed*, I'll be back as soon as I can. I'll tell you what we learn," she promised before walking out with her friends.

Abel followed Rachel to the front yard then, looking at Thomas, said, "Take care of Rachel and Mary, please.

Whatever the intent of these *Englischers*, make note of it."

"*Ya,* I will, sir. Mary and Rachel will be safe with me," Thomas said as he assisted Rachel into the buggy.

***

At the small cafe, Rachel, Thomas and Mary walked inside after Thomas tied the reins to a low fence. Thomas looked closely at both Melinda Abbott and Troy Scott and what he saw troubled him.

This Englischer *man seems to exude a feeling of superiority over us. Even though he has never met me, he acts like he is better than we are.* Thomas felt a sense of foreboding as he saw Troy's expression. *Maybe I'm misreading things or just picking up the nervousness from Rachel and Mary, but I just don't have a good feeling about this at all.*

CHAPTER FOUR

"Hey, y'all! How are you?" Melinda asked. Her friendliness seemed to belie Troy's earlier assertion of superiority over the three Amish sitting at their booth.

"We're fine. I hope you are, too," Rachel said politely. As she spoke she realized that Melinda's friendliness was the opposite of Troy's attitude. That alone made her wary.

Mary simply sat back and observed, her eyes moving back and forth between whoever was speaking.

"It's been busy, but we're both great. Listen, I spent some time thinking about our encounter yesterday. I've had some time to think about what I want to discuss with you. Questions like why you don't have phones, electricity and cars. Why don't you drive cars?"

Thomas raised his hand, indicating he would speak. "Ownership of vehicles and items of technology might be viewed as the owner seeing themselves as 'better' than those who don't. Nobody in our district owns these items, because we might become prideful. Our aim is to imitate Christ in how he lived his life. He lived simply, with few possessions. We can do the same. Besides, we have alternatives to electricity..."

"Oh, really? What do you do if you need to operate something electrical?" Troy asked narrowing his eyes at Thomas. Troy had been caught off guard by the inclusion of Thomas in the mix. He had thought he would be able to intimidate or charm the two Amish girls, and now it seemed that advantage wasn't available. Clearly, this man Thomas was intending to monopolize the conversation and that was something that Troy didn't like.

"We use vehicle batteries attached to gasoline generators. For the women in our district who make quilts, they use this method to power their sewing machines. It's the same with our milking machines. We have to comply with Indiana state law on milk production and sterilization if we sell the milk, so this is what we do to comply," Thomas stated quietly, the force of his calm personality backed the confidence of his words which caused Troy to seem to deflate slightly. Troy sat back and away from the three Amish regarding the women thoughtfully. There had to be some way to get around this brute of a man and leverage his dominance on the females.

"Well, what about computers? Can you use them?" Melinda asked her voice now more curious than anything. While the conversation seemed to have thrown off and irritated her partner, she seemed to be more and more interested in what they were saying – more like any curious *Englischer* as time passed. She listened attentively while Troy became fidgety, frowning and playing with the silverware. Melissa gently put her hand on Troy's bare arm, squeezing it slightly to calm him, but she continued to give them her full attention.

"No, we cannot. We can keep track of everything we need to do with paper and pencil, so there's no need for computers," Rachel put in softly.

"But don't some of you have websites? Like for furniture? I've seen it."

Rachel shrugged. "Maybe some do. We don't."

Troy thought this was his moment to make a move on Rachel, but Thomas leaned forward cutting him off as he went to take her hand. It wasn't an aggressive move on Thomas' part, but it was clear that he was having none of that type of familiarity with the women. Thomas started talking again, looking at Melinda. "If someone buys a computer, they risk being excommunicated from the community. We are allowed to use a public computer if we need to make a spreadsheet, but that's rare, and, if someone in our community has need of a computer for say, earning a living for their family, it must be used just for that and nothing else. Most of the time, however, we make our living in more traditional ways: baking, quilting, farming and the like."

"Okay, this excommunication thing here," Troy seized on the point leaning forward. "I thought that was limited to the

Catholics. You sayin' you excommunicate, too?"

"Yes, but with one difference. When the excommunicated person indicates they want to honestly repent, they are welcomed back. You see, our shunning – excommunication – isn't intended to be permanent or punitive. Instead, it's a discipline made from love for the person. We want them to see where they went wrong, so they can resolve to do better. When we allow someone who has done wrong to stay in our community, we run the risk of being weakened by that person who's sinned," Thomas finished talking and sat waiting for the next question.

"Man, that's harsh!" Troy said instead sitting back with a look of shock and... disgust?... on his face.

Rachel, seeing the look on his face, could not decide what to say next.

Troy gave a derisive laugh and crossed his arms. Melinda looked at him in warning, elbowing him before looking back at Thomas. "I'm sorry for that," she said softly, "I really do want to learn more about your people."

"Well, I do, too!" Troy protested. "I drove you all the way out here, didn't I?" Melinda smiled at him, but it wasn't a smile of joy; it was more a knowing smile, one of bitterness and what Rachel thought was anger. "We know why you drove me out here, Troy."

Thomas, Mary and Rachel watched this interaction with a

bit of confusion. Leaning back, Thomas directed his next question to Troy. "Why did you laugh like that? I'm explaining why we believe and carry ourselves in the way we do."

"Why don't you admit it? You're just afraid to come into the 21st century!" Troy said raising his hands and allowing them to flop back onto the table in between them.

Mary sat forward. "I want to tell you about my former beau. He is... was Amish. He came back from his running-around time and was baptized into our community church. He did so even though he felt the pull to the life and ways of the *Englischers* – that is, the non-Amish. He found work with a construction crew, and instead of using non-electric tools, he began to use the electric tools. He lived away from Hope Crossing and, well, pretty much lived like an *Englischer*. When he came back, he found our life too tame.

"I had always felt restless myself. When we started comparing our restless feelings, we decided we would move away from Hope Crossing and live among the *Englischers*. We fooled ourselves that we would still live according to our Plain beliefs. Jacob told me that, if I wanted, I could invite Rachel to come away with us. I liked that idea, so I talked to her about it. She said no. And she was blunt about it.

"She had just finished her own running-about time and knew she wanted to stay among our community. We got into an argument and she told me to leave. Well, Jacob didn't like that. He wanted me to have my closest friend with me, so he kept working on me to get her to change her mind. One day, he said time was running short for Rachel to change her mind, so we would force her to come with us."

"You mean, kidna--" Melinda asked with a look of stunned amazement on her face.

"Yes, kidnapping her. I got scared. I talked to Thomas, who talked to our parents. They told Rachel's parents and our bishop. Jacob got into an argument with our parents about leaving, and he went to Rachel's parents' house. He was about to break a window to get in and force her to leave when both of our parents and the bishop came by. They stopped him and took him to his parents' house. The bishop and deacons asked him if he was sorry for what he had tried to do. He said no, so he was excommunicated. If he comes back, and says he is ready to repent for his sins, he will be welcomed back with open arms," Mary finished.

Troy only heard "excommunication."

"So, you guys booted the dude out because of one mistake? Man, that's harsh," he said, a note of condemnation clear in his voice.

"No," Mary said. "Jacob was seduced by the lure and ease of the *Englischer* life. He was going to force his will on Rachel. When someone tries to force their will on us, that means they are not very sure of their own ideas or beliefs. We are positive of ours. We know that relying on our own ingenuity and God's grace makes us stronger."

Melinda realized how angry Mary was about her boyfriend's actions, and that she was running the risk of losing control of the meeting. She decided to take a peacekeeping role to calm down hurt feelings. She turned and gave Troy a look that said, "Back down." She turned back to the three Amish people staring at her.

"Ya know, this might be a good opportunity, not only to explore why you believe as you do, why your beliefs are so different from those who don't ascribe to them – and, maybe, we can interview you for some kind of an educational article!" Melinda finished the thought as if the idea had just occurred to her.

Thomas raised one hand to silence Melinda's enthusiasm, succeeding only in slowing her down. He wasn't sure what it was, but he continued to pick up a bad undertone from the two *Englischers*.

"Let's move slowly here. First, even if we agree to an interview, you may not be able to interview us. You might have to ask questions of our bishop or one or two of our deacons. I know the answers to all of your questions but the chosen spokesperson has to be one of these people." Thomas knew that they ran the risk of being accused of being a cult. "Also, there would be some restrictions on any type of interview."

Melinda's mouth opened and closed as she tried to come up with a rejoinder. She hadn't expected this response. "Uhh, okay. Umm, can you tell me what these restrictions would be?"

Thomas propped his elbows on the red Formica tabletop, raising the spread fingers of one hand into the air.

"First, we don't worship graven images. If someone takes a picture of one of us, this becomes a graven image, and it would be the same with a television camera."

"What about interviews by phone?" Melinda asked, looking at Troy with confusion. She had not expected this!

"This could happen. But..."

"But... What?" Melinda asked, hanging on Thomas' words.

"We don't have phones in our homes. We have a few locations where we have a phone line installed such as my carpentry shop. There's a dairy farmer down the road who has a phone installed in his barn. This means you would have to prearrange an interview time so you could get the person you'll be interviewing," Thomas leaned back in his chair waiting.

"Nah," Troy said as he crossed his arms over his chest and leaned back in the booth. "I just... I mean, you guys just sound too good to be real. Why do you avoid cameras and publicity?"

Thomas looked at Mary and Rachel then faced Troy.

"It's because we strive to be humble in our lives on a daily basis. I'm not saying it's easy, and the work is hard. It is hard and we have to recommit to it every morning. We can do such an interview as Miss Abbott has suggested, but it must happen under some very specific conditions. We want to respect our beliefs – and we ask you to respect them as well – so, if we agree to help you... educate... the non-Amish, you would need to agree to these terms. Or... no interview," he said, leaning back.

He deliberately placed both of his hands palm-down on the counter in an open position. It was his sign that this was non-negotiable. He was glad that he had come to this meeting with these two, more because Troy seemed determined to push his own agenda even past the obvious curiosity of Melinda. He didn't really trust either of them, but he definitely didn't trust Troy Scott.

Troy thought about everything Thomas had just said, going carefully through everything as he tried to find weak points where he could attack the logic. Unable to do so, he finally shrugged trying to appear indifferent. He was anything but indifferent. He was fuming. This Amish man had outwitted and outmaneuvered him and he hadn't even raised his voice. It was a fact, and it was something he didn't like, not at all. Finally with nothing left to say, he mumbled, "Whatever."

Melinda's gaze moved from Troy to the three young Amish people. She wasn't sure what had just happened, but it appeared that her attempts to regain control of her meeting were failing. With nothing else left to try, she fixed a stern look on Thomas. "Is it possible to set a date and time for this interview now, so we can come to Hope's Crossing and meet with one of these leaders?" she asked.

"It is '*Hope*' Crossing," Thomas said, looking from Rachel to Mary then back at Melinda. "Come tomorrow evening after work is done. One of the deacons or the bishop will have to make the final decision."

The meeting ended and Thomas escorted Mary and Rachel out of the diner. "I'm more convinced than ever that they're up to something," Thomas said holding the horse's reins, "especially that Troy. He doesn't like us just because we're Amish. I try not to judge, but I've met his kind before. He doesn't even hide his bigotry of our ways."

"*Ya*," Mary said. "I don't get a good feeling about this or their interest in us. Let's talk to the bishop, and let him make the final decision, though."

"Even Miss Abbott, Melinda, she seems to have an ulterior motive," Rachel said. As she spoke she rubbed her thumb along the hem of her apron. "I... had a dream last night. Jacob and these *Englischers* were all mixed up in it. I think God was trying to tell me that the *Englischers* want to make us do something that is against our faith."

Mary leaned forward and stared at Rachel across Thomas' torso. "You, too? I had the same kind of dreams last night! I woke up and wrote them down," she said. "We need to really be careful, Rachel. We have to pray because we are being given a message."

CHAPTER FIVE

They returned to the Troyer home, and Thomas sat down to sip an icy glass of lemonade and speak to Abel and Barbara about their encounter at the diner.

"*Nee*. I don't like this. I agree – they're up to something and it isn't going to be good," Abel spoke up as Thomas finished relating their meeting. He leaned back in his chair thinking, absentmindedly rubbing his beard. "We try to teach when asked, but many times the asking covers something less than honorable. This has that same feeling, and if the man is any indicator, they don't have the learning about our community and way of life as the only thing on their agenda."

Rachel and Mary gazed at each other communicating silently. It was something that they had done since childhood, a combination of knowing each other so well and silent cues they shared with each other. Rachel nodded and took the lead.

"*Daed*, I had nightmares last night about this. These *Englischers* and Jacob were in my dreams. Mary had the same kinds of dreams. We agree – they are up to something, but we don't know what," she said to her father as her gaze moved from Abel to Mary and back again.

Barbara had been silently listening to the conversation. "Do you think they want to try and make us change, and if so, why here? And, if that's not what they're trying, what are they about?"

"I don't know, Barbara. It... it just doesn't feel right. Thomas, you handled it right. Letting them know that an interview is possible, but that the bishop or the deacons would make the final decision was inspired..." Abel rubbed his fingers over his mouth as he thought. "Now that I think about this some more, they may be thinking of saying that we are some kind of sect or a cult, and that we exercise too much control over our children."

"That would be ridiculous, but it has been said in the past. We are neither a cult nor some kind of secret sect. We raise our children in the way of God, and we exercise the same control that all parents have over guiding our children to adulthood."

"We can only wait and pray for God's guidance. I think you handled things just right, and I believe that all things done in the dark come to the light."

Thomas and Mary left the Troyer home. Their ride home was quiet as both wrestled with their private thoughts and fears. At home, they sat down with their parents.

After hearing what Thomas and Mary said, John sat back and crossed his arms over his lean stomach.

"*Ya,* son. They are up to something. What it is, I don't know, but it won't be good. Mary, make sure you stay close to Rachel at market days. I don't want you being made a target by these people. Most *Englischers* are good people, respecting us and our ways. Others... to borrow a term they use... not so much. I will talk to Abel Troyer, and we will go talk to Bishop Bontrager and let him know what has developed. Let us begin to handle this situation. Thomas, I will need you to go with us tomorrow before you begin working on your current order."

***

Immediately after breakfast the next day, John and Thomas drove their buggy to the Troyer home. Speaking to Abel, they decided it was high time to bring the bishop in on the issue.

At the Bontrager home, all four men sat outside discussing the recent developments. Thomas explained what he had learned from Mary then about their meeting with the two *Englischers.*

"What they're saying... how they're acting, makes me feel suspicious. Thomas, do you have any ideas of what they might want?" the bishop asked pacing on the porch. He was thinking about the incidents that had happened in other Amish communities.

"Bishop, the only thing I can think about is that they want

to compel us to use modern conveniences – vehicles, electricity, computers, cell phones... all of it. They had a difficult time understanding just why we refuse to rely on these conveniences." Thomas said leaning against the wood fence. "The woman, Melinda Abbott, seems to have an interest in our ways and culture, but the man, Troy Scott, was almost rude and dismissive of what we had to say. In some parts of the conversation, he openly mocked our ways and expressed absolute disbelief in what we were saying. All in all, he was quite unpleasant."

"Hmmmm. Okay. You are right. The deacons and I will meet with Miss Abbott and Mr. Scott. Did they say what purpose this article would serve?"

"'Educational,' or so they said," Thomas replied with a skeptical look and tone. "It seemed more about why we refuse to rely on technology. They... worry me. More than Jacob did when he was planning to kidnap Rachel. I wish I could put my finger on it, but it's just an overall feeling that they are not here just to write an article."

"Well, at least, Thomas, if Jacob truly repents, we can welcome him back. These *Englischers*, though," the bishop said, shaking his head. "Not knowing for sure what, if anything they have in mind worries me. Okay. I will meet with Miss Abbott and Troy Scott tonight. However, Thomas, I want you, your *daed* and Rachel's *daed* there as well."

All three agreed to be present for the meeting, and later that evening, the four Amish men met Melinda and Troy at the agreed-upon time and place.

***

"So, Bishop... is that what we call you? You're not wearing ceremonial robes or anything!" Melinda started out with an attempt at humor, but the joke fell flat as none of the Amish men even cracked a smile.

"No. We practice a Plain lifestyle, meaning that I am no higher than the least of the people in Hope Crossing. I follow exactly the same rules, if you will, as anyone else. Now, about..." Bishop Bontrager paused.

Troy had pulled out a large camera and was changing various settings on it. "Mr. Scott, no. I cannot allow you to take a photo of me or any of these men. If, however, you wish to take a picture of us from the back we can allow that. Or you can take a picture of the barn or one of our buggies. However, no photos of our faces, please. I thought Thomas had informed you of our feelings about photographs," the bishop finished shaking his head.

Troy let out a loud, throaty sigh of disgust. Melinda looked at him in warning, and then returned her attention to the bishop. "So, about these conditions that Thomas mentioned. Is he right?" she asked, rubbing Troy's muscular shoulder with one hand trying to calm him down. He reminded Thomas of an abused dog driven to attack and held back by its owner. He seemed more than just edgy; he seemed spoiling for a fight with them but just couldn't figure out how to get it started.

"Yes, he is. No photos, no video. Because we have only a few phones scattered throughout the community, any appointments we make would have to be made face-to-face; our interviews would also have to be in person."

Troy had set the camera down with its lens facing the four Amish men. He sat back feeling restless and angry at being denied a chance to catch them out in a lie. These people annoyed him with all their pious commitment to religion and faith. The ban on taking photos was just another reason he didn't like them. *I don't know why Melinda is so obsessed with these losers.*

"Excuse me... sir," he butted in. "Just why do these restrictions exist?"

"Because we believe in practicing humility, just the way Jesus Christ did, possessing certain items would lead us away from our path. If we owned cars, for instance, or phones, cell phones, dryers, washers or computers, we would be in danger of becoming prideful at what we own. We would believe that having these things puts us above others who don't have them. We believe this is a sin. Therefore, for every one of us to embrace a Plain life makes it possible for all of us to grow closer to God," the bishop spoke clearly and slowly, fixing Troy with a stern gaze.

Troy had been following everything Bishop Bontrager said. Again, he tried to find a weak spot in the bishop's argument but, unable to do so, slumped in his seat.

Melinda paused, appearing thoughtful and solemn as she looked at Bishop Bontrager. "Sir, if you would consent to an interview, we will follow and respect any conditions you set." As she spoke, she clasped her hands tightly seeming to take a prayerful attitude.

Troy felt a sudden rush of excitement. *Yes! She's taking them where we want to go! Go for it, girl!* He masked his excitement with an attitude of boredom at the whole conversation. He wanted to use any resulting interview to get to Amish youth in the Elkhart area – those exploring the world and their options, to question their faith and commitment to the Plain life. *One of those girls made a huge mistake, talking about that "running-about time," because we can use that to get these kids to see just how... backward their lives are.*

Melinda waited patiently as Bishop Bontrager made his decision.

The bishop nodded. "Okay. We will have the interview under the conditions I confirmed for you," he said, looking at John Schrock. "If possible, I would like to meet at John Schrock's home and farm. It's on the edge of the Hope Crossing district and more convenient to our guests." Because the Schrock farm was also on the edge of the district, it would be easier to escort the guests away from Hope Crossing, if it proved to be necessary.

"*Ya,* that is fine. I will talk to my wife and let her know. I'm sure we can have a light snack ready as well," said John. Once the decision had been made, the two *Englischers* had no excuse to stay around. They drove off as the bishop, Thomas and John remained in their group.

"We will be at your farm tomorrow evening after supper," the bishop promised John. With that decision made, the three split up and went their separate ways.

CHAPTER SIX

Back in their apartment, Melinda and Troy sat on their sofa and discussed the day's accomplishments.

"Troy, you very nearly blew everything up by trying to take a picture of them! That bishop dude was something serious," Melinda said shaking her head. "No ceremonial robes, that long beard, no mustache, the same kind of clothing that his 'followers' wear... what do you make of that?"

"The no-mustache thing makes 'em all look... weird. 'Followers.' I think you have it right, Mel. Now, how'd I nearly 'blow everything up.' hmmm? All I did was to start changing my camera's settings," Troy challenged Melinda.

"Look, Troy. They say they can't have pictures taken of them because of that 'graven images' thing from the Ten Commandments. Google it and see what it says. I just wonder if they're actually some kind of cult. Do they really follow these rules willingly? Just wish I could remember what that girl called it," Melinda commented as she jotted a note to herself to ask about the name of the rules. "Okay, what I'm going to do is write up a set of questions that I'll ask them. That will keep them going on the education article angle. We must get closer so that we can rescue their children."

"We need to approach those kids who are taking that break and exploring our world," Troy suggested taking a healthy slug from a bottle of beer.

"Yeah, I agree. You know, now that I think about it, we shouldn't leave the women out of this. I want to talk to those girls we met at the Amish market – Rachel and Mary – and find out what Amish life is like for females. Dressed like they are, I wonder if they are forced to be modest. Y'know, we might be able to convince them that they are suppressed, Troy," Melinda said, pointing her pen at him for emphasis. "Not only will this make a great exposé on this particular community, but it will allow us to help those kids out, too. The more of them we rescue and return to a humane way of living, the better."

"Our group lives to release these children from bondage. All cults have victims and these people are no exception." Troy looked out the window at the passing traffic below. "Remember what that cult my mom joined did to me. I don't care what they're called; they're a cult and we are here to rescue them."

Sometimes Melinda wondered about Troy. He seemed like he was re-rescuing himself every time they liberated children from the various cults they found around the country. He had the same fanaticism that cult members possessed, except he was obsessed with freeing the children from cult bondage. She often thought his fanaticism was like a drug addiction; he relived, through those they rescued, the victory and high of his own liberation from that hell hole he called his childhood.

She knew he would never stop. It made him a perfect partner in this enterprise. It also troubled her that one day he would go too far.

CHAPTER SEVEN

Bishop Bontrager sat in his kitchen thinking about the two *Englischers*. *On the surface, the woman seems to want to learn about our beliefs and culture so they can educate others. But... I was getting some... undertones that I didn't like. They have some kind of ulterior agenda, and I don't know what that is. Lord, you know what is in our hearts, even those who may not view us in a positive light. I am asking for your help before tomorrow's interview.*

The next morning, Thomas was busy at work on a dining room set some *Englischer* customers had ordered from him. Seeing how much work he needed to do, cutting the wood, he moved to his large gasoline generator to check on how much gas he still had. Back at his saw, he was about to switch the machine on when he heard a distinct female sob. Turning around, he saw the female *Englischer*, Melinda Abbott. She was very well turned-out in a skirt, brightly colored shirt and blazer with heels – and she was in tears.

Thomas shoved the big length of wood farther up on the table and walked to Melinda. His instincts told him to be cautious, but he still felt protective.

"Miss? What's wrong?" he asked walking towards her.

"I'm sorry for intruding on your work! We… Troy and I… were working, taking pictures of farms like your bishop suggested." Melinda sobbed several times loudly to punctuate her point. "We got into a ho – horrible argument!"

Thomas wrapped his hand around Melinda's arm and guided her to a long bench at one end of the shop. "Tell me what happened," he asked. His brow was wrinkled – something wasn't adding up, but what was it?

"Well, we were taking pictures, like I said. He aimed his camera at a young woman – one of your Amish women. The woman saw him pointing the camera at her, and she told him not to take a picture, but he kept aiming at her. I put my hand on his shoulder to make him stop. Well, Troy just blew up at me!" Again, Melinda sobbed – but she didn't wipe tears off her cheeks which clicked for Thomas. He realized Melinda wasn't really crying, but not wanting her to know that he'd figured her out, he nodded in sympathy. "Go ahead."

"He told me he doesn't think y'all are really as good as you are. That you believe the life you live in. I tried to tell him that you are, that you really believe what you say you follow." Another fake sob. "I was skeptical at first, but now, I have a better understanding of why you choose to live such a hard life.

Do you really force your children to live such a hard life, too? That's what he wanted to know. I tried to tell him that living Plain wasn't a death sentence, and he said he thought you were a cult. He seems obsessed with that thought, and that your children are all brainwashed and that's why you stay. What should I tell him?"

"We are not a cult, and living Plain is not a nightmare. We do not brainwash our children. Quite the contrary, they make their own decision about whether they want to join our community and get baptized or not."

"But he said you excommunicate those who don't want to join your community. Don't you think that they feel forced?"

Thomas thought for a moment considering his next answer. He said this, he said that, but who was asking the questions? As if on cue, Melinda sobbed again. "These have been our rules for as long as we've been a community. Those who decide to leave can return at any time."

"Yes, but if they don't, well, what about their families. Don't they miss them?"

"Yes, I'm sure they do, but –"

"Of course, these are his questions, not mine." She took out a tissue dabbing at her dry face. "I know you have your ways and rules. He's just so, well, obsessed. I really had to stop him from breaking your rules."

"Thank you for telling me this, and I'm glad you stopped

him from taking that picture. I'm sorry to rush you off, but... I have a big order I'm working on. And I need to think about what you've just told me," Thomas thought about needing to say a prayer and to quickly alert the bishop to what had just happened.

"Oh! Okay, I'm so sorry for disturbing you! I'll just go back to my office... and I'll see you this evening. Thank you for listening," Melinda said with a shaky smile, dry eyes and an obvious quiver in her voice.

Thomas shut the door of the shop, bracing his hands against his work table saying a short prayer asking for help about the conversation. Crying without tears was acting, but he was more disturbed by her questions about the children and brainwashing.

***

Troy drove slowly through Hope Crossing. He was not angry because he had not gotten into an argument with Melinda. They had agreed that she would find Thomas and tell him the story about the faked argument, so she could ask him questions about the Amish children and observe his responses.

Whistling a random tune, Troy drove towards his second target. This was the conversation and data gathering stage, and while he would much rather be in the final stage where they were carrying out their objective, he felt they needed to be absolutely sure prior to starting anything. He found the Troyer home with little trouble, strolled up on the porch and knocked on the front door. He put on his best "I'm no threat" smile and waited for someone to answer.

Barbara Troyer opened the door wide, not used to strangers coming to her front door. She closed it slightly when she saw the *Englischer* standing there, but she kept her smile.

"Good morning. My name is Troy Scott, and I met your daughter the other day at the Amish market. I wonder if I might have a few words with her. If you need to supervise, I am quite comfortable with this." He threw that last line in to further throw the woman off her guard – at least he hoped that would be the case. After a moment, she opened the door further allowing him to enter her large, spacious kitchen. She offered him a seat, and went to get her daughter.

"Rachel. Mr. Troy Scott is here. He needs to talk to you. I know you're still busy with the baking, but it shouldn't take too long," Barbara said mistaking Rachel's head shake and thinking it had something to do with her busy day.

Rachel sighed and washed her hands and walked towards Mr. Scott, sitting down across the table from him next to her mother. They stared at him expectantly.

"Miss Troyer, thank you for agreeing to meet with me," Troy said with a wide smile. He carelessly set his messenger bag down next to him on the kitchen table – inside, he had hidden a tiny tape recorder, which he had switched on as he followed Mrs. Troyer into the kitchen. "I just wanted to ask you a few questions ahead of our interview this evening.

Melinda and I were talking about the direction we wanted to take our interview in, and she asked me to speak with you about what your daily life is like. What you do, what your dress and bonnet mean, things like that."

"Mr. Scott," Rachel began politely, "my mother was not aware of the rules set up by the bishop and elders about this interview. I should not be talking to you without their permission." She felt her mother tense next to her. She had been unaware of what had transpired earlier which is why Rachel brought it up. "This is highly irregular."

"I'm sorry. I did not mean to intrude or break any rules. I'm just doing a little background work so that Melinda and I can write a fair, unbiased view of what Amish life is about. I just need to ask a couple questions so that I know which way to steer the interview." He placed his hands on the table palms up as if his fate was in her hands, shrugged slightly and gave her his most charming smile. Rachel didn't return the smile but looked thoughtful. She again noticed his green eyes, irises outlined in smoky blue. They were heavily lidded, sleepy looking as if he was deliberately attempting to charm her with his eyes. She didn't care for the feeling at all and looked away out the window as if gathering her thoughts.

"I don't think it would do too much harm if you answer a few questions, Rachel." Her mother looked hesitant then added, "and if he asks something untoward or unseemly, I'll be here to put a stop to things."

"All right then." Rachel still wasn't entirely comfortable with the arrangement, but she was raised to be courteous to everyone and that feeling was warring with her inclination to be cautious.

"So, your dress?" Troy prompted breaking the impasse.

"Well, you've heard us talk about Plain living. That involves dressing modestly and not calling attention to ourselves. The women all wear similar-style dresses with either long sleeves or sleeves that reach the forearms. The necks are high and the skirts hit at least mid-calf. No bright colors and no buttons..."

"Excuse me? No *buttons*? So, how do you keep them closed?" Troy asked in confusion.

"We use safety pins or hook and eye closings, functional but nothing that would adorn our clothing. The men don't have buttons on their pants or shirts for the same reason. We wear simple, plain shoes. The women wear prayer *kapps* to hide our hair. The men wear straw hats in the summer and wool hats in the winter, because covered heads are a sign of humility,"

"What about your work days? I know we've discussed this more than once, but how do you, for instance, do all that delicious baking with no electricity?"

Rachel rose to show Troy the diesel generator connected to their stove and oven. "While we don't use electricity from the power grid, our *Ordnung* allows us to do this. Because my baking is my business, I need to be able to bake large amounts of goods every week so I can sell them and help my family out."

"Wow. This is really cool," Troy said. "Question, and I ask this with the most respectful intent – but how do you feel about these rules – this '*Ordnung*' you live under?"

Rachel thought carefully before responding. Her instinct told her to tread carefully. "The *Ordnung* is in place to help us follow a Christlike life. There are some, like Mary's former beau, who... chafed... under our *Ordnung*. I see it as a tool, Mr. Scott. I'm not perfect. I make mistakes and these rules remind me of why I am to love and imitate God. And, it's not always easy for me to follow our rules."

"Well, have you ever considered leaving all these rules and regulations behind?"

"During my *rumspringa*, I had a chance to make that choice, and I chose to stay a part of the community."

"Isn't that like brainwashing?" Troy pressed. She might be one of the young people who needed rescuing.

"No, I chose to come back to my community and live in this fashion. Nobody made me come back or stay."

"Don't these rules stifle your individuality?"

"No, not at all. I am an individual who is part of a larger community. Each community has its own set of rules, and what our *Ordnung* tells us we can and can not do is different from another community's *Ordnung*. So, you see, it's up to each individual community to decide how they are going to follow Christ," Rachel hoped she was making a good impression and representing her community well. "I live my life, respecting the message in my Bible. I dress modestly out of respect for my parents, my community and God."

"Haven't you ever wanted to take that hat off, let your hair down and run freely through the fields?" Rachel's mother gasped and prepared to rise.

"It is all right, *Mamm*." Rachel placed her hand on her mother's arm stopping her mid rise. "Mr. Scott, I know you may not understand this, but I don't want to call attention to myself. I believe that Christ died for my sins and for all those sins of my family, friends and everyone outside the Amish communities. This set of rules isn't written. It's something that we, as a community, discuss periodically."

"But, aren't the children stifled in their freedoms and creativity by having rules imposed on them whether they like it or not?" Again, Rachel felt her mother tense. This conversation was not going well.

"All children need rules and guidance, Mr. Scott. Even *Englischers'* children have rules to live by. And, it is not something that is imposed on us. It is a group effort. We may make a change on something, such as allowing a community member to work with computers at their place of employment. The *Ordnung* governs our daily lives just as the state laws and ordinances do. How we cook, work and earn money is all covered by the *Ordnung*. Out of respect for the temples that are our bodies, the *Ordnung* tells us how we can court."

"How about political involvement? Can you run for, say, the school board?"

"No. We're not allowed to run for any political office, divorce, sue anyone, use electricity from the public grid, or own or operate cars or televisions," Rachel ticked off each point on her fingers as she spoke.

"Wow. Da– oh, I'm sorry. Nearly forgot there," Troy said, having the grace to blush. "How about the military? Are you pacifists?"

"We can't join the military. We aren't pacifists, but we are conscientious objectors."

"How about medical care and medications?"

"We are encouraged to seek medical attention and treatment when it's needed."

"Okay, you can't own cars. What do you do when you need to travel long distances? Say, hypothetically, you need to take a sick kid to the state capital, because that's where the best medical care is?"

"We can hire a driver to take us. There's nothing in the *Ordnung* that doesn't allow us to get a ride when we need one."

"I've asked you this before. You can't use electricity. How

you get along without that is mind-boggling for me. So, what do you do if, say, your boyfriend has to cut lots of wood for his carpentry work?"

"Just like I do with my oven, he uses a diesel generator and an inverter to power his saws."

"Okay. Thank you for bearing with me. One last question, please, then I'm outta' your hair. This... *Ordnung*... thing is pretty comprehensive. How... Let me think how to phrase this..." Troy gazed off into space with his jaw pillowed in the palm of his hand appearing to think deeply. "Okay. How do you *really* feel about these rules? Don't they make you feel like a little tin soldier with a wind-up key, sending you on your way?"

"I'm not sure I know what that means, but please realize we have grown up with these rules guiding and shaping our lives since we were young. More often than not, I'm grateful they are there."

"Okay, I think that's it... yeah, I've covered everything I needed to ask you," Troy said giving her another engaging smile.

Rachel smiled slowly back; she trusted him less now than she did before, and she hoped she hadn't said anything that could be misconstrued or twisted. That whole thing about the *Ordnung* and following the rules was disturbing to say the least.

"I want to thank you for helping me to understand. I was pretty skeptical yesterday. Those rules, when you talked about them, sounded pretty... well, strict." He shook Rachel's hand letting his thumb make a slow circle on the back of it, releasing it, and following her mother to the front door. "It was very nice talking with you again, Rachel." He turned, bowing slightly, giving her that green-eyed gaze that had so captured her attention at the market, another smile then a turn and he was gone.

Rachel didn't know a lot about men; she had led a sheltered life and even when she had gone out into the world, she had pretty much stayed to herself. Mary had called her an aberration; she should be out partying and having fun doing all the things she couldn't do when she lived at home. But Rachel had gone into the world only to learn her trade to perfection, and after a period of intense study, she had been grateful to return to her community.

She was also pretty sure that Mr. Troy Scott was flirting with her; all that smiling, the thing with her hand, leaning in with his charm and beautiful green eyes. It was another sign of disrespect, because he knew she was with Thomas and that they were planning to be married. Or, did he? Rachel couldn't remember if that part of the conversation had ever come up. She would ask Thomas to make it clear when they met the next time.

Her love for Thomas was unshaken even though she found Troy Scott attractive. He was definitely not her type;

something about him just rubbed her the wrong way and she was somewhat afraid of him. God did not put these thoughts and feeling in her without a reason. And all things in the dark would come to light in due time. Of that she was sure. And, that was certainly a very odd interview. Warning bells were going off in her head. What had he done that was odd? Beyond the questions, he had done something else that made no sense. She replayed the talk with him in her mind.

"*Mamm*, wait a minute..." Rachel's smooth brow crinkled as she tried to put her finger on why the interview was so peculiar. *His bag. He took no notes!*

"*Mamm*, how could he remember everything we talked about? He didn't even take any notes!" Rachel walked to the refrigerator removing the cookie mix she had been working on.

"Daughter, I don't know. Maybe he just has a really good memory!" Barbara said as she began working on that night's supper.

Later that evening, Thomas stopped in with the tale about his encounter with Melinda. "Rachel, she was sobbing, but made no tears. I didn't see her wipe tears from her face one time," Thomas paced back and forth on the back porch.

Rachel's jaw dropped. "Thomas, Mr. Scott came by today and 'interviewed' me. He asked me all about the *Ordnung* and how it guides our lives. He asked me if I ever feel 'restricted' by these rules and I... I told him that, at times, I do. Thomas, we talked for nearly an hour and he didn't take any notes. But the questions he asked were more about how I really feel about the rules, how the children live with the rules and are restricted and having the rules imposed on them. It left me feeling very uncomfortable. My *mamm* let him in, because she didn't know about what happened before with the bishop."

"Rachel, I think we were taken. Where's your *daed*?"

"Inside. Why?" Rachel stood and scurried to catch up to her taller, longer-legged beau.

"Come with me. He needs to hear what happened," Thomas muttered. "Sir, something happened to both Rachel and me." Thomas sat down in front of the older man, resting his elbows on his knees and placing his chin in both hands, and then explained the events of the day.

"Well, I think they got what information they could out of you," Abel said, looking at Thomas and Rachel.

"Sir, I think we need to go see the bishop about this, let him know what happened. Would you go with us, please?" Thomas stood to leave.

"Ya. I will. Your horse is still hitched to the buggy. We'll go in yours." The three left right away. "Barbara, lock the doors and close the windows. Do not allow anybody into the house." He didn't think they would return again, but you never know with people with an ulterior agenda. They were trying to get information in sneaky ways, and God only knows how they would twist it to their own needs in that article.

"*Nee*, I won't," Barbara began to secure the house, closing the curtains and locking the door securely after they left,

At the bishop's house, Rachel and Thomas told him what had happened to the two of them. "They contacted you to get as much information as they could before tomorrow's interview. All we can do is pray and ask for his guidance that we say the right thing to avoid what they are trying to do to us here in Hope Crossing, It will probably be another less than truthful article; our community has weathered worse and as long as that's as far as it goes, we can just wait it out." He gazed at them through his wire-rim glasses giving them a reassuring smile he did not really feel.

"Bishop, what do *you* really think they are trying to do?" Thomas asked. He wasn't sure the bishop would have an answer, but the bishop's response threw him.

"Thomas, at best they will write a less than complimentary article about our people and culture. At the worst, and I pray this isn't the case but I've heard about it happening before, they will try to take our children by tempting them with worldly goods or by force if necessary." Bishop Bontrager sighed deeply. "They ask too many questions, and I remember when it happened in the community in Garland, couple years back. Two people came to do an interview; they were pushy and obnoxious. They never caught them, and I wonder if these two might be the same people. There was also a theory going around that there was a group of people who were all about 'freeing children from cults.' The fact that our community is not a cult hasn't changed their minds or slowed them down."

CHAPTER EIGHT

The following night the bishop came to the Schrock house to meet with Melinda and Troy. He came to the house having prayed for divine understanding the night before. The insight he gained told him that all of Hope Crossing would have to band together to resist the evil that both Melinda and Troy might personify. Before the meeting, the bishop had met with each deacon from the district – Deacons Stutzman, Hershberger and Mast – asking them to be present for the interview. The Troyers had also come to the Schrock home. Bishop Bontrager wanted them all there so the *Englischers* could see that their community was as one.

At the end of the interview, Melinda and Troy shook everyone's hands, gathered their equipment and left escorted by the bishop. Everyone else stayed in the large kitchen waiting for him to return.

"Well. This was... interesting," said the bishop sitting down. "Let's talk about the threat they represent. Thomas and I spoke yesterday, after both he and Miss Troyer were approached by these *Englischers*. He asked me what I thought they were trying to do, and I told him that they may be attempting to gain access to our community in order to cajole, influence and even kidnap our children – those who are in their running-about time who are considering returning to the community and those who will soon begin this phase of their lives. Miss Troyer was 'interviewed' by Mr. Scott about the *Ordnung*. Thomas was approached by Miss Abbott, who appeared to be crying but not producing tears. We allow our children to experiment and try different practices before they are baptized. It's their decision to come back or not when their *rumspringa* is done. However, these people, if they're part of the group I suspect they are part of, will upset the natural order of things."

"Bishop, I think we need to go out to every family with running-about youth and warn them of this development," said John Schrock. "We should include the families whose children will soon enter their own *rumspringa*."

"Let's talk. How would we accomplish this?" The bishop was inviting suggestions.

Thomas leaned forward. "We need to tell them about Miss Abbott and Mr. Scott. Warn them not to let these two into their homes – or near their children."

"Yes, that is a good suggestion. We need to tell them in such a way that alerts, but does not frighten them," said the bishop leaning back in his chair.

Rachel was getting a sick feeling in her gut. "Bishop, Mr. Scott was discussing Amish life and the *Ordnung* with me. I don't know for sure, but I think he was getting material from me so they can twist it and persuade our *kinner* to leave. He asked me how I feel about the presence of the *Ordnung* and its effect on my life..." Rachel trailed off with a look of apprehension on her face.

"I think you're right, Miss Troyer," the bishop said giving her a compassionate look. "I don't want any one of you to speak to them anymore. They will know that we have figured them out, but that's all we can do. We cannot use force in any way. If they try to use force against us... we will call the *Englischer* law enforcement." The bishop gazed for several long seconds at each person in turn.

"I have a suggestion," Thomas said, raising one hand. "I know we don't like to rely on the law enforcement of the *Englischers*, but we are all getting the same bad feeling about Mr. Scott and Miss Abbott. We all know they don't understand the reasoning for why we have the *Ordnung* and why we follow it. They will understand the sheriff's department better. If these *Englischers* try to do anything, we have only ourselves to rely on. We don't have weapons. I hope and pray that the *Englischers* won't try anything, let alone anything that would hurt any of us, but, just in case they do, the sheriff can deter them. We can have them here quickly if we need them here. Maybe they can make them stay away from Hope Crossing, too."

Everyone in the small group discussed Thomas' suggestion. The bishop looked from person to person, Rachel included then slowly nodded his head.

"Okay. We will go to see the sheriff in the morning. It will be me and the deacons only. Everyone else, go about your days and we will let you know what we learn," said the bishop, tapping his forefinger into the table for added emphasis.

"*Ya, denki.* This is good," Thomas said feeling a little less worried.

When Rachel and Thomas were finally alone, Rachel broached the delicate subject that she dare not bring up in front of the bishop or deacons. "Thomas, I think Mr. Scott is flirting with me. He may not be aware that I am spoken for, but yesterday when he shook my hand goodbye he made a really strange gesture on the back of my hand. He also invades my personal space whenever he can. He smiles but it makes me uncomfortable."

Thomas was quiet for a moment before responding. "Thank you for telling me this. I will definitely have a word with Mr. Scott if it continues. In the meantime, I will keep myself between you and him until this interview business is complete. Chances are after that we won't see either of these *Englischers* again."

***

The next morning the three deacons and the bishop drove

away from Hope Crossing and went to the sheriff's office.

"How may I help you?" the sheriff asked, concern and confusion evident on his face. Amish seldom visited his office; they usually handled their own business within their community.

"Yes, it is unusual, sheriff. However, we are confronting a situation that, itself, is 'unusual.' A pair of *Englischers* introduced themselves to two of our members at a recent Amish market day. From that meeting they conceived of the notion that they could interview several of us for some kind of an 'educational' newspaper article. I spoke with them and they got their interview. I learned afterward that each of these people had visited two of our young adults, obtaining more information than what I had given them. Sheriff, none of us has a good feeling about the intent or motives of these *Englischers*."

"Have they done anything to anyone in your district?" The sheriff leaned forward, retrieving a pen from the holder on his desk. He started writing on a yellow pad taking notes about what they had just said.

"No. No they have not. But the man was driving around our community while the woman was in the carpentry shop of one of our members. She was supposedly crying about some kind of disagreement she had with her friend. I say 'supposedly,' sheriff, because young Mr. Schrock told me that the *Englischer* woman sobbed, but had no tears coming out of her eyes. In short, she was faking her crying."

"Well, given that they haven't done anything that breaks any local, state or federal laws, there's nothing I can do about these people. Are you sure they aren't just curious? Maybe they truly do just want to inform other '*Englischers*' of your lifestyle?"

"Unfortunately, all we have is our gut feeling that something isn't right. No, they haven't done something, sir. But they asked several... probing questions of Miss Rachel Troyer that make us worry that they will cast their article in such a way that encourages our children to question their faith and leave," the bishop leaned forward to make his point, his cool gray eyes intense, a frown evident in his furrowed brow.

"Or that they will physically come to Hope Crossing to seek out our teenagers and persuade them to leave," Deacon Mast put in, his face equally intense with worry.

"Unfortunately, there is nothing I can do right now, and unless they physically try to take your children, they've broken no laws. However, if they do try to interfere with your parenting, daily life, routines and worship, then we can act. But until then, the most I can do is instruct my deputies to drive through Hope Crossing and look for them. Now, do you know what they drive?"

"Mr. Schrock told me they drive a dark-gray Hummer. Even patrols through will help. Thank you!" Bishop Bontrager stood, shaking hands with the sheriff.

"I wish I could do more, but the law ties my hands," he said. "However, we will increase patrols through Hope Crossing, never fear."

CHAPTER NINE

When the deacons and Bishop Bontrager returned to Hope Crossing, they had a brief meeting. "Let's just keep a close eye out for these two people. Look for a large, dark-gray Hummer. You've seen the two *Englischers* at the interview. If you see them, greet them. Make it clear to them that we are watching them. Don't make them leave. They want to describe us as a cult and making them leave would confirm that for them. Just... keep an eye on them when they are here."

"Bishop, we should ask the Schrocks and Troyers to watch out for them as well. They know who to look for and they know why we are all concerned," Deacon Stutzman, a stout, gray haired man put in.

"Yes. That's true. I will talk to them and get their help." By that evening, John, Thomas and Abel had agreed to help watch out for the two *Englischers* as well.

While he was driving to the Troyer home, Thomas' eyes scanned the landscape, looking for the Hummer; he sighed with relief when he didn't see it.

When he arrived at the Troyer's, he and Rachel decided to take a buggy ride so they could take advantage of the warm, sunny evening.

"Rachel, the bishop and deacons have me, my father and your father watching out for Miss Abbott and Mr. Scott. If you see them or encounter them, let your father or me know right away. We can't make them leave, but we can figure out what they are up to," Thomas said holding the horse's reins easily as they rode.

"Yes, I will." Rachel sighed. "I just feel so... guilty that I gave Mr. Scott so much information about the *Ordnung*,"

"Rachel. Rachel, look at me. We trust because we're honest. Right? And, when we encounter someone who's not trustworthy, it's not easy for us to catch that right away, so they can get what they want with very little effort. It's not your fault," Thomas' eyes unlike Mr. Scotts were blue eyes filled with sunshine and mirth. To Rachel they twinkled as if with golden light and every time she saw him, it made her smile. He took Rachel's hand in his own and placed it on top of his leg as they rode.

Rachel, feeling the hard muscle of Thomas' thigh under her hand, made her a bit breathless, and she knew beyond a shadow of a doubt that although Mr. Scott was attractive, it was Thomas who owned her heart. "I just don't want them using the information I gave them for a bad purpose."

"If you see them, don't confront them. Just turn and walk in the other direction, and then let your *daed* know. Okay?"

"*Ya.*" Rachel smiled at her beau, trying to get her pounding heart under control. He was so handsome, his hair the color honey against his pale skin and his whimsical, sparkling eyes.

"One thing I've been thinking, Rachel. I think you and Mary could help out with this. We should visit families in Hope Crossing – those families with children about to begin, or who are in, their *rumspringa*. We need to let them know what's been happening and what we suspect. But I want to talk to my *daed* first and have him talk to the bishop. If he likes the idea, we can all spread out and talk to a few families to ensure the safety of their *kinner*," Thomas glanced at Rachel to see her reaction.

As he hoped Rachel was smiling. "*Ya*! We can do this. It lets the families know what we suspect and we aren't putting anyone in harm's way,"

The next day Bishop Bontrager and the deacons visited Thomas and John.

"I like this idea. We need to start tonight." The bishop always seemed in control to Thomas – stout, strong and wise beyond his years. His graying beard made his face seem more mature, but his smile brought a twinkle to his eyes just as the furrowing of his brow signified the seriousness of the situation. The bishop never seemed grim except at the deaths of community members, but he did convey a sense of somber authority at times like these that was both reassuring and firm.

"That's fine. After we both finish working we can start visiting families," John replied.

"Bishop, I think we should also have my sister, Mary and Rachel help us out. A woman's touch can go far towards preventing overreactions," Thomas said.

"*Ya*. We should also divide the district so we each have a few families to visit," the bishop said, rubbing his mouth.

Over the next several weeks the Schrocks, Troyers, Bishop Bontrager and all three deacons fanned out across Hope Crossing, visiting families to spread their warning. Almost uniformly parents said they would be watchful for the *Englischers*. When John Schrock and Bishop Bontrager talked to two teens, the boys said they had already been approached by either Troy or Melinda.

"*Ya,* Bishop. A blonde woman talked to me." Samuel King was a lanky boy with honey blond hair, brown sparkling eyes and generally smiling and of good cheer, but when he spoke of his conversation with the *Englischers*, he looked visibly upset. He frowned as he spoke, brows lowered, face slightly reddened, speech staccato-like and clipped.

"Samuel, what did she say?" The bishop looked startled and worried.

"That we are a 'cult' and we have the right to live our lives more freely. But Bishop, I like my life! I believe in my faith and in the *Ordnung*! I told them that I don't want to talk to them anymore. I know I should have been more polite, but they wanted me to come with them. I told them I wasn't leaving my community." Samuel looked down scuffling his feet.

"Thank you for telling me this. Did you tell your parents this?"

"No, my *daed* has been feeling sick, and I don't want to worry my *mamm*. She has worried enough without learning this." Samuel stopped looking down and brought himself up to his true height of 6'1" before continuing. "We don't have to worry them with this, do we? I have been handling the bulk of the farming work while my *daed* is sick, and I don't want him to worry that I might be whisked away in the night."

"No, Samuel," Bishop Bontrager reassured him. "But from now on, stay close to home. It would be a good idea for you to only go places with your *mamm* or *daed* when he feels better, hmmm?"

"*Ya, denki.*" Samuel smiled at the bishop. "They would have a hard time getting me to go anywhere I don't want to go, too." While his voice sounded strong, there was a tinge of fear in his eyes as he spoke.

At the home of Herschmanns, Caleb their teenage son admitted to seeing the *Englischer* three times in the last week. "He came to the fields where I was working on the fence. He just showed up out of nowhere driving the huge car he owns." The boy seemed intrigued by the car the man drove. "We talked about cars and how engines work; stuff like that. Nothing out of sorts, just how car engines work and why some cars have great pickup and others don't."

"Caleb! Why didn't you tell me?" his mother asked in a scolding tone. "You know…"

"Mrs. Herschmann, to be fair, Caleb didn't know the risk this man poses," Bishop Bontrager quickly interceded. "While you shouldn't be talking about cars, Caleb, I can see how these things would be tempting to a boy your age."

"I'm sorry, Bishop Bontrager. I was just curious, that's all." His eyebrows rose up slightly, wrinkling his forehead. His eyes glistened with unshed tears, and he tightened his mouth into a taut, rigid look. "I'm sorry. I didn't know."

"It is very likely that this man has targeted your son for removal from Hope Crossing. If you think it would help, you could send him to stay with his older brother and sister-in-law for a few weeks. We – the deacons, two families and I – are keeping a lookout for these *Englischers*.

"We will make sure they don't get to any more of our children. Mr. Herschmann, Mrs. Herschmann, I can take Caleb to his brother's house right now. The *Englischers* don't know where he lives and Caleb would be safer."

"*Mamm, Daed*, I want to go. I don't want to get taken away against my will. I love our community and my life. I admit, I am curious about cars and engines, but that's all." He gave them a pleading look.

"Pack your things and take your schoolbooks. Go with the bishop, son, and we'll see you in a few weeks," his father decided, placing his hands on his son's shoulders. "Curiosity is natural, and there was no harm done. We know you want to stay in our community, and this man has been sent to test our faith. Of course, he's going to prey on the young who are curious and easy to lead."

Fifteen minutes later, Caleb was packed. After hugging his younger siblings and parents, he boarded the bishop's buggy and went to his brother's house.

While they were visiting families in the district, the Schrocks, Troyers, deacons and the bishop all kept looking for the *Englischers*. Because they kept watching while they were out running errands, it didn't look like they were on the lookout.

These measures resulted in the sudden lack of availability of Amish children to Melinda and Troy. Over the next few weeks, as they came into Hope Crossing, the children were suddenly and mysteriously absent – especially the teenagers.

CHAPTER TEN

"Man, I don't know where those kids vanished, Mel. It's like they've been sucked up by a huge sinkhole," Troy commented as he collapsed onto the comfortable couch.

"I don't know, either. School's still in session. Well, at least we got to those two boys. Maybe we convinced them to think about things. Maybe, when they start that running around time, they won't come back," Melinda said as she stretched her tired back. *But why did they suddenly disappear? Where are they? At home? It's not like we can knock on doors and ask to speak to them!*

"Melinda. It's time to write that P.R. piece. Like an exposé, making these people out to be like a cult. I'll help you send it to as many news organizations as possible, and then they will realize just who they're messing with," Troy gave her an ominous glare almost like a snarl that sent shivers down her spine. Who was Troy Scott?

"I'll get that started after we eat," Melinda said as she

flopped onto the couch next to Troy. "One thing. I have the notes I took during our interview. Do you have notes or a recording of your conversation with the Troyer woman?"

"Tape recording. No notes," Troy said as he pulled the small recorder out of his messenger bag.

Melinda took the recorder then froze.

"Uhh, *no notes*? You just hid the recorder and... talked?"

"Yeah, is there a problem?"

"Well, duh! Yes, there is! I think I just figured out why we can't find any kids to talk to! They wised up to us, Troy – because you messed up by not taking notes!" Melinda yelled at him as she got up and started pacing.

"Well, sorry, Miss Reporter! It's not like I can write, listen and talk at the same time! Besides, how do you know that's why the kids are suddenly out of sight?" Troy asked challenging Melinda.

"Look, Troy. Those kids were out there, playing, weeding, going from farm to farm, just hangin' out before our interviews. Now? For the past week, we haven't seen hide nor hair of even one teen. Just the little kids, who're too young to reason things out for themselves. That's what it has to be! You wouldn't have needed to take real notes. Just plop a pad in front of you and make little squiggle lines and make it look like you were writing," Melinda said. "Man, I don't believe this! You may have blown us out of the water!"

After they ate in a glowering silence, Melinda set her laptop on the table and read through her notes. Slipping earbuds into her ears, she listened to Troy's recording of his conversation with Rachel Troyer. Troy had banged out of the house after gobbling down a fast dinner. The house was silent and Melinda had to satisfy herself with a small nod and a comment to herself about the good quality of Troy's questions to Rachel.

"Guess I'll apologize to that big lunk and let him know his questions are actually good!" she sighed to herself. Drumming her fingers on the computer desk, she assumed her favorite thinking position: leaning back in the leather executive chair and slinging her shapely legs to the surface of the desk and linking the fingers of both hands behind her head. Once she had developed the bones of an attention-grabbing lead sentence in her mind, she leaned forward and began writing. Referring to her notes and Troy's recording, she wrote out the basics of a first draft for the article she and Troy would use to pull the Amish into the 21st century. Several hours later, she stretched as she heard Troy's key scratching in the lock. Turning she saw him stumble in.

"Hey, I want to apologize to ya. You may not have taken notes, but you actually conducted a great interview," Melinda said.

"Yeah, whatever," Troy mumbled. "I'm going to bed. I'm pretty wasted." He veered and stumbled as he made his way to their bedroom.

Back at her computer desk, Melinda looked at Troy's back, surprised at his rejection of her overture. Becoming angry, she saved the document and slammed her computer shut, then flopped onto the sofa and switched the television on.

Waking early the next morning, she stuck her head in the bedroom and, in a loud voice, announced that coffee was on. She grinned as she saw Troy jerk then moan. Out in the kitchen, she turned the volume up on the morning news show.

There. That loud perky news announcer should... Man, he's really hung over! Melinda thought as she heard Troy retching. *His fault. No sympathy for him.* Melinda closed her eyes as she savored the hazelnut creamer in her coffee. Setting the cup down, she decided to spray her strongest perfume on, just to tweak Troy. Coming back into the kitchen, she set her coffee mug next to the computer and began working. She smiled as she heard Troy moan.

"Sick, my love?"

"Shut up." Troy poured his coffee and began to sip it gingerly, hoping his stomach would behave. Thirty minutes later, he realized Melinda was wearing a particularly strong perfume. "Lord, woman, wash that smell off! It's making me sick!" Setting his coffee mug down, he ran back to the bathroom.

In the living room, Melinda rooted through her purse and pulled out a sanitizing wipe then wiped it over her neck and wrists. Ten minutes later, scent-free, she was working when

Troy came out.

"Sorry. Didn't know you'd be that sick," she told him. "I wanted to tell you last night that you actually did a pretty good job on that interview with Rachel, even with no notes. I'm sorry I blew last night."

"Now, she says it. 'Kay. Thanks, apology accepted. I'm going to work on this hangover. When – if – I feel human today, I'm going to try and find more kids later on," Troy poured more coffee.

"Okay. I'm going to keep working on this. When you can read without pain or vomiting, I'd appreciate you looking at it."

"Yeah. I'll check through it. Uh, don't forget to stress the cult angle," Troy said, leaning back on the couch. "Oh, man, turn that woman down! Her voice is like a drill in my ears." Troy grimaced trying to keep his stomach under control.

Melinda grabbed the remote and lowered the volume. *Point made. I'll be nice now.*

By noon, Troy had recovered sufficiently so that, with sunglasses on, he could venture out of the condo.

"I'll be back by dinner," he told Melinda.

"Okay. I should have most of a first draft by this evening," she responded, turning around to watch him.

***

One week later, Melinda printed out a draft of the completed article.

"Hey, Troy, take a look at this please. I think you'll like the changes I made," she said, handing the warm pages to Troy.

Troy read through the article carefully. As he did, he nodded and made small noises of agreement in his throat. As he finished reading it, he nodded with a smile, handing the pages back.

"I like it. Excellent. It's perfect as-is. Copy it to your letterhead and I'll help you send it out to as many outlets as we have available," he said. After faxing and emailing the article to press outlets on the national, regional, state and local level, the couple was gratified to receive communication from several of those outlets interested in running the story.

***

Abel and Barbara Troyer stopped at a newsstand as they saw tall headlines trumpeting "access" to a "reclusive Amish cult in northern Indiana." Abel, alarmed, fished out several coins so he could buy a copy of the paper.

"You read while I drive, Barbara. Let me know what that article says. From that headline, it won't be good," he said, loading bags of purchases into the back of the buggy.

By the time Barbara had finished reading the heavily slanted article, Abel was livid.

"We are going to stop at the Bishop's house before we go home. He must know about this now," Abel said in a low, rumbling voice.

At the bishop's house, the three sat around the table and discussed the article.

"I will go and buy copies of as many different newspapers as I can find. I want to speak to the deacons about this because it is bad. This makes it look like we imprison our children and brainwash them. Thank you for bringing this to my attention. I want to go and buy different newspapers – those that have this article. I want to see what they say."

Abel and Barbara went home, leaving the bishop to drive quickly to Elkhart and buy as many different newspapers as he could find. By the time he finished, it was nearly the end of the day and he had a pile of papers from seven different outlets. Back in Hope Crossing, he stopped at Deacon Mast's house.

"We need to meet with Deacon Stutzman and Deacon Hershberger," he told Deacon Mast, as he handed him three of the newspapers. "Take a look at the article then we will talk to them."

One hour later, they were sitting in Deacon Hershberger's kitchen, reading and discussing the articles, all of which painted the Hope Crossing community as a cult.

"This has gotten to the point that we need to talk to the community," the bishop said.

"*Ya,* we do. We have a meeting this weekend. Do we say something at this meeting? Or…"

They discussed the need for a meeting then the pros and cons of informing the community about the existence of the article and its purpose in harming their community. In the end, they decided they would have the meeting as planned then, during the lunch fellowship, they would bring up the article.

***

That Sunday's meeting was held in the Kings' barn, and after the meeting ended and the men were rearranging the benches and tables, the bishop went to his buggy and pulled the newspapers out. Returning to the barn, he gathered with the deacons.

As adults both old and young sat down or milled around, the bishop raised his voice to get the community's attention, then launched straight into the cause of the unusual meeting.

As everyone realized the import of the article, a low, rustling murmur went through the group and people looked at each other with their mouths gaping open. Rachel recognized her words, even though they had been altered just slightly. She put her face into her hands and shook her head.

Standing, she spoke. "Bishop, I was explaining to Mr. Scott how the *Ordnung* helps us live our lives and worship God. They make it look like I'm saying we're a cult! These are my words – but, at the same time, they aren't. They changed them." When the final shift of people had eaten and cleaned up inside the King house, children and their parents left, leaving the older youth and young adults staying behind for the singing.

Rachel stayed, but she wasn't in the mood for very much socializing – she still blamed herself for her innocent part of the situation. After the singing ended, Thomas sat with Rachel on the back porch of her parents' house. They were talking about the newspaper articles and the charges that the Hope Landing Amish were a cult.

"Rachel, I am going to be keeping a watch on your parents' home. I don't know for sure, but I suspect that Mr. Scott and Miss Abbott are likely to return there," Thomas looked protectively at Rachel.

As he finished speaking, Barbara Troyer came outside.

"Rachel, those *Englischers* are here and they want to talk to you," she said. Her face was pale as she thought of the damage the article could do to them.

Rachel shook her head emphatically, causing the ties of her prayer *kapp* to swing wildly back and forth. "*Nee, mamm.* I am not going to talk to them. They lied about me!" She stayed on the back porch with Thomas, trembling with the force of her anger.

Barbara shut the back door and returned to the front door.

"No. She does not want to speak to you. I cannot blame her

at all. Now, leave our home," she ordered, her gray eyes snapping with anger. Before they could respond, she shut and locked the door in their face.

Outside, Melinda and Troy seemed to leave, getting into their Hummer and driving a distance down the road. Instead, they parked the SUV to the side of the road and began walking back to the Troyer house. Sneaking from the road to the side of the house, they made their way to the rear of the house, where they spied Rachel and Thomas talking and eating cookies.

Rachel spied the *Englischer* couple lurking at the side of the porch. Glowering at them, she grabbed the cookies as Thomas swung around to look. Seeing them, he glared and grabbed the pitcher of lemonade following Rachel into the house. He shut and locked the door.

Troy ran onto the porch and began knocking insistently at the door. He kept knocking even when nobody answered.

Inside, Rachel, holding her arms tightly crossed, said, "Do not answer that door! *Mamm*, where's *Daed*?"

"He ran out as soon as you came in," Barbara said.

Abel had left through the front door going to the barn where he called the sheriff. Ten minutes later, the sheriff showed up and, directed by Abel, went to the back porch, where he surprised Troy and Melinda.

"You have to leave. The family doesn't want to talk to you, and they don't want you here," he told the couple. "If you don't leave, I'll be forced to put the two of you under arrest." Standing solidly on his wide-spread feet, he crossed his arms and looked calmly at the two dressed in their fashionable clothing.

Troy threw his hands in the air and released a gusty sigh.

"Okay, okay! I just wanted to see how they liked our article!"

"Well, given they don't want to talk to you, I would guess they hate it. So, leave. Now."

The couple gave up and left.

Walking back into the kitchen, he told the Troyers that he didn't think Melinda and Troy would stay gone for very long.

"I'm going to have my deputies' patrol along this road and others. If they do try to come back, we'll arrest them for trespassing, but that's as much as we can do – unless they try something really stupid," said the sheriff.

It was dark and Thomas had long since gone home. Rachel and her parents were already upstairs in bed. Troy and Melinda decided to return to Hope Crossing to see if they could talk to Rachel. While they were on the front porch knocking at the front door, the sheriff's deputy passed by.

Seeing the white of Melinda's dress like a bright beacon, he stopped, calling the report in. Getting out of his car he ran lightly up the steps to the porch.

"Excuse me. The sheriff has us doing a patrol of this area and he said that this family doesn't want to talk to you. Why are you here?"

"Officer, we just want to talk to them about the article we did," Melinda said, giving the deputy a beaming smile.

"No. Ain't happening." Along with his partner he pulled his handcuffs from the back of his service belt. "You're under arrest for trespassing and harassment. Turn around."

After Melinda and Troy turned around, both deputies locked the handcuffs on and placed a hand around the upper arms of both suspects to lead them to the patrol car. Just before Troy entered the vehicle, he turned, one foot in the car and looked angrily at the large, two-story house.

"I'll get you! I'll take your kids away from you!"

Hope Crossing families were further convinced that the two *Englischers* really posed a threat to them and their children. Parents all across the district responded by increasing the level of protection around their children. Parents picked up their children at school – no child was allowed to walk home from school. Children, regardless of their ages, were only allowed to play in the back areas of their homes. Instead of allowing them to play out after dark, parents began requiring them to come in before the sun went down.

CHAPTER ELEVEN

Because the two *Englischers* were in jail, it was the quietest time in the area for the Hope Crossing families. Melinda got out of jail first – because of the threat he made, Troy was housed in the county jail, in custody of the county for several weeks more.

As the days passed, and Troy stayed behind bars, his anger grew exponentially. After he was finally released, he told Melinda they would have to act soon.

"Where are they in the largest numbers?"

"At school... but..."

"No. No buts. We'll grab a few kids at the school," Troy said looking fixedly at Melinda as she drove.

"Troy, all we want to do is let them know they don't have to follow this lifestyle! There's no need to kidnap any kids!" Melinda tried to divide her attention between the road unfolding in front of them and her angry boyfriend.

Oh, my God, is he going to kidnap or – heaven forbid – kill a kid? Licking suddenly dry lips, she gave Troy a calming smile. "Honey, all we need to do is connect with the older kids and let them know they're free to pursue their own..."

"NO! Melinda, dammit, it's gone past that. The plan's changed. We're grabbing some kids." Troy faced the front, glowering through the windshield and cutting the conversation short.

At home, Melinda paced in the living room realizing after a moment or two that the heels of her shoes made too much noise. Yes, it was a nonsequitur, but she always focused on the random when she was this upset. She kicked them off and continued pacing in her bare feet. She was scared – really scared.

Kidnapping indiscriminate children was not the plan. All she and Troy had wanted to do was rescue kids from the Amish cult by showing them the error of their ways. They should make their own choice to leave, and they would provide transportation to those who wanted to leave. Like that Caleb boy; he showed real interest according to Troy in the outside world. They would be there if he decided to go on *rumspringa* and not come back. She had no plans to snatch Caleb from his family if he didn't want to go, but now Troy was all about just snatching kids and running with them.

I have to get rid of him. If he's changing our plan like this,

I'm changing my plan, too. I'm going to continue to rescue all children from any authoritarian, suppressive regime by talking to them and showing them a different way. But before I do that, I have to get rid of Troy. I can't be involved in a crime! Another couple he had been involved with had gone down that road, and even the group didn't want them around.

CHAPTER TWELVE

Troy became more and more obsessed with the idea of revenge against the Amish of Hope Crossing. Angry because he and Melinda had been barred from returning to the small community, he spent much of his time hand-drawing maps of the community from memory. In all of their movements through the district, they had become comfortable with where different buildings were located. Even with no street names, Troy and Melinda had learned to navigate Hope Crossing by using landmarks, such as the Troyer home – and the school house.

As she worked on her P.R. articles for other clients, Melinda became ever more alarmed at Troy's state of mind and his single-minded focus on getting back at the Amish.

"Troy, we're starting to run low in our savings. I don't want to see it dip any lower, so do you know of any engineering work coming your way?" Melinda posed the question in as relaxed and unconcerned mode as she could ignoring his surly mood and pages of handmade maps.

"Damnation, Melinda! Can't you see that I'm busy trying to get us back on track for getting those kids out of that cult? No! I've turned down some assignments. I want to finish this," Troy's voice had a testy edge, his eyes somewhat glazed with anger and something she couldn't quite put her finger on. Insanity? Obsession?

His posture and countenance seemed angry, but there was something else in his look that disturbed her to the point where she became silent just watching him. "Besides, you need to remember this – we will be rescuing these kids, either en masse or one by one. We'll take them from the school. Somehow."

Melinda felt even more frightened. Her biggest concern was Troy's state of mind and inability to focus on his beloved engineering. Second was their dwindling bank account. While she had invoices outstanding, they would only replace a portion of the money they had spent in the past two months

I have to warn them what he's thinking of. Only, dammit, they don't have phones in their homes. There's no guarantee that I'd be able to get someone if I called a phone in a barn or something. Not that I know any of those phone numbers. Oh, God, what can I do? What have we done?

Two days later, Troy leaned into the study/office. "Hey, Melinda, I'm going to scout out the roads around Hope Cross... No, don't worry. I won't go into that place. I'll be back in a few hours."

Melinda sat for fifteen minutes before she made her decision. Driving to the sheriff's office in Elkhart, she didn't know what she was going to say, but she had to say something. Troy was seriously going over the edge, and she didn't know when he would strike. She wanted none of this kidnapping children plan, and there seemed only one way to stop it: bring in law enforcement to stop him.

"Sir, I know your deputies arrested us. We were wrong to do what we did. I've come to realize that, sheriff, but Troy..." Melinda gasped, trying to control a sudden impulse to cry. "Troy... won't let go of the idea. He's going to try and take them one by one – the kids – or he'll kidnap them as a group!" Passing her hands over her face, she realized she sounded crazy and disjointed. Forcing herself to calm down, Melinda looked straight at the sheriff. "Please, sheriff. You have to believe me."

The sheriff leaned back in his chair, eliciting a loud, protesting creak from the large spring. He looked at the wild-eyed woman with tears trailing down her pale cheeks.

"Miss Abbott, I'm sorry. We arrested you not one month ago – and now you're saying you've had an epiphany? A change of heart? Sorry. I can't believe you. I've had criminals try to divert my attention in the past – I think that's what you're up to right now. It won't work. Please leave or risk being arrested again."

The harsh words slammed into Melinda's gut. Getting up

slowly, she knew she had no choice. Troy would be home in a couple hours anyway, and she didn't want him figuring out that she was suspicious of him.

"Thank you anyway, sir. I just hope... you'll believe me soon," she said quietly as she walked out of the office. Turning to face him once again, she said, "I'm going to do everything I can to convince you that I'm telling the truth. Troy is becoming dangerous."

"Miss, the only way I'll believe you at all is if you call off this campaign of yours against these good people. The Amish are peaceful, and they live their lives respecting the rights of others. They don't try to impose their religious beliefs on others, which, sad to say, isn't something practiced by other 'Christians,'" The sheriff stood behind his desk indicating the door.

Melinda left, hearing the sheriff's last words echoing in her mind. At home, she tried to work on other P.R. assignments, but found she was too distracted. Giving up work for the day, she wandered around the apartment. Finally, she decided to go outside and get some sun. Feeling hungry later in the day, she decided to try her hand with some comfort food. After she put a pan of lasagna into the oven, she returned to wandering the apartment. Troy came home as she was walking from one room to the other, waiting for the timer to ding.

"Hey. How was your day?" he asked.

"Eh. Not great. I tried to get some work done, but couldn't.

I made dinner instead," Melinda said, leaving out her trip to the sheriff's office.

"Why you so distracted?" he asked.

"I'm... just angry because we were arrested. That was just... wrong," Melinda lied, hoping to get more of Troy's state of mind.

"Pssshh! Same here. Those Amish have a stranglehold on the sheriff's office. I'm glad you're seeing that now," Troy said, stalking to his office, where he pulled out a map and began making changes to it.

Melinda nodded. "Yeah. Whatever. I'll let you know when dinner's ready."

"Yeah. Just bring a plate into my office and I'll eat there. I have a lot of changes to make anyway," Troy tossed over his shoulder.

A few minutes later, Melinda pulled a steaming pan of lasagna from the oven. Dropping tossed salad and a cut portion of the hot pasta onto a plate, she stabbed a fork into the lasagna and stuck a napkin and bottle of salad dressing under one arm, taking everything into Troy's office. She set the plate and dressing on a side table wordlessly.

"Don't forget that's there. I don't want to waste food," she told Troy.

Back in the kitchen, Melinda served herself and ate then

cleaned up the kitchen. She checked to see if Troy had eaten anything. She sighed gratefully when she saw that he'd eaten everything. After stashing his plate and fork in the dishwasher, she returned to her office and closed the door.

How to get the sheriff to believe me? What did he say about their religious beliefs and practices? Something about not imposing on others. Waitaminnit. Hold the horse, I think I might have the answer!

She pulled up the article on the Amish on her computer then took her mini-recorder out of her desk. Inserting her earbuds into her ears, she turned Rachel's "interview" on and listened to it closely. This time, however, she tried to keep her mind open, remembering what the sheriff had said. When she got to the part about Rachel's feelings about having to live in accordance with the *Ordnung*, she listened to that portion several times.

Oh, my God! The sheriff is right! Rachel doesn't always like having to comply with the Ordnung, but she knows she'll be more successful living her life as Jesus did...

Another question bothered her – about proselytization. Rachel had talked about the Plain life she lived. Did that have something to do with how they refused to evangelize? Did they feel that proselytizing would call attention to themselves? *My God, that must be it! They – she was telling the truth. Now, I wonder if I can get the sheriff to believe me. He was right. They don't force themselves or their beliefs on the community-at-*

large. I wonder... this "running-about-time" – what is it, really? What's its intent? Maybe some targeted research...

Several hours later, Melinda came back to the world and realized that it had gotten dark inside and out. Switching her desk lamp on, she thought about the scholarly research she had just finished reading.

We were so wrong. They don't force their will on their kids or on the public. They allow their children to decide for themselves if they'll return to their community. My God. I have to stop Troy. Somehow, I have to stop him!

Stretching kinked neck muscles, Melinda hurried into the darkened living room and kitchen. Empty. Trotting to Troy's office, she knocked and opened his door.

"What? I'm busy here!" he growled.

"Troy. Stop. Please, stop! We made a huge mistake. I just re-read my article and listened to Rachel's interview – you know, the one you did? They don't force their beliefs on anyone, not even their kids!"

"Yeah, we made a mistake. We should have grabbed some kids when we had the chance. Now we're barred from entering... *What* did you just say?" Troy pinned Melinda with a sharp look.

Melinda rubbed her hands together.

"Troy, we have to stop! They aren't a..."

"SHUT UP! We know what we know about them and they *are* a cult! Leave me alone!" Troy raised his voice at Melinda, something he never used to do.

Melinda gasped, shocked. She got mad at him, swirled around and slammed his office door as hard as she could. With the echoes of the slam reverberating in her ears, she yanked a closet door open and pulled out blankets and a pillow. Making up a bed in her office, she muttered to herself.

"...yell at me like that. Well, fine. If he won't listen, then the consequences will fall just where they'll fall. I'll find a way of contacting the sheriff somehow." Before switching the office light off, she logged onto the Internet to see if she could find a way of contacting the sheriff's office.

"Okay, click the 'contact us' link. Good. He has an email address." Clicking on this, Melinda quickly wrote an email to him, outlining what she realized and learned through additional study of her notes and the Troyer recording.

"Sheriff, I know you don't believe me. I blame myself, because my actions make it look like I'm dishonest, with an axe to grind. I'm really afraid that Troy won't let this go. He's determined to take several children from Hope Crossing. I want to stop him. I hope I can get you to believe me. Thank you, Melinda Abbott"

Before logging off, she erased the search from her search history and deleted the email from her "sent" box. Kicking her shoes off, Melinda shut the office light off and slipped in between the blankets.

The days passed slowly as she waited for a response – any response – from the sheriff's office. Feeling like the waiting was making her as obsessive as Troy had become, she decided to do some more research on the Amish – this time, solely for learning. Finding several knowledgeable websites, she read. The more she read, the stronger her realization that she and Troy had been grievously wrong about the motives of the Amish. A quiet realization began to assert itself in her spirit after a few days – as she read, she felt herself drawn to the peace the Amish beliefs and lifestyle represented. Looking up, she realized that her laptop monitor was easily visible from the door of her office. Not wanting Troy to see what she was doing, she decided to rearrange her office so she would be the only one who could view the screen – anyone looking at her desk from the window or doorway wouldn't be able to see it. After scooting her desk around, she sat down, panting slightly and resumed her research.

"Hey. Wow, you finally took my suggestion and rearranged your office. Nice. Listen, I decided you were right the other day," Troy said.

Melinda felt a thrill inside. "About... what? I was talking about several things," she said slowly.

"Taking some engineering jobs. You've brought in quite a few, but our checking account has taken quite a hit. I got a call from an old client and he wants me to go out to Montana for a couple weeks, work with him on a computer engineering contract he just got. It's big and he needs my help. I just booked a flight and I'm leaving in three hours. Don't worry about taking me to the airport in Indianapolis. I'll drive and just park my car there in the long-term parking. Gotta go," said Troy, bounding to Melinda who had stood and walked from around her desk. Leaning down, he gave her a quick kiss.

"You'll be gone for how long? That's great that he wants you!" Melinda said, trying to catch up to Troy's train of thought.

"Two weeks, maybe three. I'll stay in touch. Hey, while I'm gone, keep trying to find a way we can get to that school at Hope's Crossing. We still need to follow through on our plans. I'd do it, except..."

"You'll be gone. I'll be researching, don't worry," Melinda said. *You just don't know that I won't be researching how to grab kids.*

Twenty minutes later, a newly energized Troy had finished his packing and blown out of the house, speeding to Indianapolis to catch his flight west.

After he flew out of the house, Melinda opened her laptop again. She continued her research, jotting down notes or bookmarking websites for later reference. In the back of her mind was a question – how she could repair the damage she and Troy had done. By the time she looked up again, the shadows in the quiet room were lengthening. She jumped as her cell phone rang. Seeing Troy's name on the screen, she picked up.

"Troy? Have you arrived yet?"

"Yeah, just got to my hotel room. Have you been researching how to get onto that community's land?" Troy asked.

"I've been doing research all day long. I did go out for a while and looked around, but... really don't want to be arrested again!" Melinda said, closing her eyes at the lie.

"What's wrong? You sound... odd. Like you're not really all there," Troy said with suspicion.

"Headache. I'm going to take something and lie down for a while before I eat," Melinda said. Feeling restless, she began pacing around the office. "Sorry, Troy. I can barely see right now. I think going out in the sunlight after spending all morning long online really did a number. I'm glad you got there. Thanks for calling me! Bye." Melinda quickly hit the "end" button and set the phone down, exhaling a relieved breath at the same time. She felt ravenous. Wandering into the kitchen, she looked for something to eat. She decided on a salad. Switching the television on, she watched the news then, when it was over, started scrolling through the channels.

As luck or fortune would have it, she found a program about the Amish on an educational channel. Lifting her feet, she settled in, getting comfortable as she became engrossed in the program. During a commercial break, she checked what would be shown on that station after the Amish program ended.

"Wow, cool! Another Amish program! Can't believe that I'm enjoying this, but I am," she muttered to herself. After watching three hour-long programs, she decided to watch the late news and go to bed.

Melinda found herself in Hope Crossing – wearing the traditional long-sleeved, modest dress and a prayer *kapp*! What was going on? She was in the kitchen of an Amish home, making a meal, using a stove connected to a diesel generator. Her dream went through several other scenes. What was the most shocking was when she found herself at an Amish worship service. Waking suddenly, Melinda sat up and switched the light on.

"What... was that? Me? In an Amish kitchen, wearing the bonnet and a long dress?" Melinda realized that, as shocked as she was, she felt... less worried than she had felt in the past few weeks. Even waiting for the sheriff to respond to her email, she didn't feel as worried as before she had begun her research.

After lying back down, she drifted back to sleep, waking when her alarm clicked on. She heard the morning radio announcer talking about the day's weather and commute. Stretching, she got up and decided she needed to do more research. Maybe she *could* repair some of the damage she and Troy had done – with or without him.

Two hours later, she grabbed her phone, thinking it was

Troy.

"Miss Abbott? This is the sheriff. I'm responding to the email you sent a couple weeks ago. I don't know how, but you've convinced me that we need to talk. I'd like to meet with you somewhere away from Elkhart. I don't want your boyfriend knowing that you've contacted me, do you understand?" he asked.

"Definitely! I deleted my search for how to contact you then I deleted my email to you from my 'sent' box, so I don't want him knowing, either," Melinda said.

"Very good. Now, I have some time this afternoon before our shift change. Can you meet me at a park or something?"

"Yes, I can! Thank you! What time and where?" Melinda asked, holding a pen over a writing pad.

"About two miles outside town, there's a park by the creek. Meet me there at one this afternoon."

"I know where you're talking about. I'll be there, by myself," Melinda promised.

At one on the dot, she stepped out of her SUV, looking for the sheriff. Seeing him on a park bench, she walked toward him.

"Miss Abbott, how are you? Before I begin, have you respected the order to stay away from Hope Crossing?" the sheriff asked fixing a stern gaze on Melinda.

"Yes, I have. I don't want to be arrested again."

"And your boyfriend? What about him?"

"He has, too. But he's trying to find a way to get back on and get to the school so he can grab some of the youth," Melinda said in warning. "Sir, I don't want violence used to stop him. But I do want him stopped. Those families don't deserve what we were planning," Melinda said. As the words came out of her mouth, she was stunned.

Hearing her words, the sheriff looked at Melinda. His gaze seemed to measure her and he seemed to be thinking of the sincerity of her words. Shifting position, he began to speak.

"Okay, what's going on? I need to know everything. We can obtain search warrants, so don't leave anything out," warned the officer.

Melinda sighed. She was relieved and scared, by turns.

"Okay. I went through my notes and Troy's interview with Rachel Troyer. This time, I didn't go through them with the intent of slanting things against them – I listened so I could learn. I realized that we've been wrong all along. I tried to tell Troy and he yelled at me and told me to shut up. So, I did and started doing my own research. I... we've really done a lot of harm and I realize that now. I won't go into the peace I feel when I research now, but it's there. Sir, I just want Troy stopped. I don't want to grab kids any more. You were right – they don't force their beliefs on others. Oh. Troy's out of town for two or three weeks, on an engineering job he just got," Melinda finished, out of breath and with her heart pounding. *Oh, please let him believe me! Please, God!*

"Go on. What, exactly has Mr. Scott done to achieve his goal?"

"He's been drawing maps of Hope Crossing from memory. He hasn't gone back, but he wants to find a way to watch the school and get kids. Somehow," Melinda said. She gulped back sudden tears, praying that he'd believe her. "He left them at home and told me to study them. When he gets back, he wants me to give him ideas."

"Maps. Miss Abbott, I want you to go with me back to the office. I want to bring some additional men in on this. Let's go."

At the sheriff's department, Melinda followed the sheriff to a small office with beat-up furniture. "Here's a bottle of water. I'll be right back," the sheriff promised, walking from around his desk. Closing the door, he went to another part of the building. Two minutes later, he came back with two deputies.

"Miss Abbott, tell these deputies just what you told me. Everything," the sheriff ordered.

Melinda took a sip from the bottle of water she'd been given. Wetting her lips, she repeated her story. She waited as the deputies and sheriff discussed their thoughts and theories. She sighed in relief. She had done all she could do. It was now in their hands – and God's – as to what would or wouldn't happen next. She listened closely, realizing that they believed her. She closed her eyes in relief.

"Miss Abbott, you've convinced us that Mr. Scott hasn't dropped his plans to grab children from Hope Crossing. But this means you're in danger. From your boyfriend. You say he's out of town and we believe you, but we don't know if he's cooked up his trip to trap you or us. Now, I'm sending another deputy to bring back some leaders from Hope Crossing. They need to know what you've told us. It'll take some time for them to get here, so you'll need to wait," the sheriff warned her as he sat on the edge of his desk.

"I'm fine with that. I'll wait. But... he called me from Montana..."

"Did he use a hotel phone or his cell phone?" the sheriff asked.

"His cell phone," Melinda said slowly, realizing what he was thinking. "Oh, my God. I left my computer and all my notes at home!"

"No worries. We'll get everything for you. Give me your house key and I'll have someone get clothes, your toiletries and your electronics. But you cannot go back home," he said a new stern note entering his voice.

Melinda nodded, taking her house key from the ring. She gave him her address and a female deputy left to get everything she needed.

Melinda began waiting. One minute then another slowly ticked past. Finally, nearly one hour had passed when the office door opened. The deputy walked in with one of the Hope Crossing deacons. A younger Amish man walked in with the two. Melinda, seeing the younger Amish man, felt her heart thump as her breath whooshed out of her throat. She saw a tall, sturdy young man with light-brown hair and gentle, dark-brown eyes.

"Miss Abbott, this is Deacon Mark Mast and his son, Steven," the sheriff said. "My deputy should be back before long with your things." He motioned for the new arrivals to sit down. "I know you've told us everything several times, but would you mind repeating it just one more time?"

"As many times as I need to be believed," Melinda said. She took a long swig of the cool water, trying to moisten her dry mouth. She turned to the two Amish men and repeated what she had already told the law enforcement officers.

"Please, believe me. We came to your community with... with bad intent. It's only in the past few weeks that I've realized that Troy really intends to do harm to you and your young people. *I don't want that to happen.* I... misstated what Miss Troyer told Troy when he was talking to her. I made it sound like she was saying you are a cult. I realized a few days ago that you don't force your way of life or beliefs on others. That what we have been planning to do is just that – forcing our beliefs on you, and that is wrong. Please, please, believe me! I want to stop something very bad from happening to your children!" Melinda pleaded as her voice trembled.

Deacon Mast leaned toward Melinda.

"Why did you plan to take our children, Miss Abbott?"

"We... honestly believed that your community was a cult. But when I listened to Rachel Troyer's interview again, I realized how wrong we were. Troy... Troy still wants to sneak into Hope Crossing, and he wants to kidnap as many teens as he can," Melinda finished as she wiped the tears that cascaded down her cheeks. She looked from one Amish man to the other.

Steven Mast was now gazing at Melinda with what looked like respect, if not acceptance, in his eyes.

"*Daed*, I think she's telling the truth. I can't find any deception in what she's saying," said Steven as he looked at the deacon.

Melinda, hearing this, closed her eyes in relief.

The sheriff nodded in agreement as well. "Miss Abbott, if Troy is so determined to continue with your plan, he could be dangerous, not only to the community, but to you, too. I have a very small force, barely adequate to patrol and protect the county. I don't have the manpower to protect you in your apartment," he said, shaking his head and rubbing his hands over his eyes.

"Sheriff. We practice forgiveness. We have forgiven Miss Abbott for her actions. It's clear she has repented. She can stay with us at Hope Crossing with my family and me – but she must comply with our beliefs," Deacon Mast said, leveling a look at Melinda.

"Anything. I'll do anything!" Melinda said, as her heart pounded. Still, the news that her boyfriend could pose a danger to her stunned her. Still... she thought back over the past several weeks. That new urgency in Troy to snatch Amish kids. As she thought of living at Hope Crossing and hiding out, she wondered if she could leave her conveniences behind. Would she be able to use her computer? Would she be allowed?

"Miss Abbott, because you came to me about what Mr. Scott is planning, you placed yourself in danger. At this point, you have no choice. You'll have to take leave from your job," said the sheriff, counting off points on one hand.

"I'm... I'm self-employed. I can take a short break from finding and writing P.R. articles," Melinda said feeling numb.

Someone knocked at the office door.

"Enter!" the sheriff ordered.

The female deputy came in, bringing suitcases and Melinda's computer.

"Nobody there, sir. It looks like Scott's out of town, just like Miss Abbott said," the deputy reported.

"Excellent. This gives us time to get you acclimated to Hope Crossing. Now. We'll need to hide your car. I'll authorize a space inside our garage. Your vehicle will stay there until we catch up to, and stop, Mr. Scott," the sheriff said.

"We'll take you back to Hope Crossing with the Masts," the deputy said.

CHAPTER THIRTEEN

At the Mast home, Melinda was welcomed to the home.

"Miss Abbott, we will protect you here. Because you admitted to what you did and what has been planned, we have forgiven you. I believe you now understand our beliefs and lifestyle," the deacon said, removing his straw hat.

"Thank you for taking me in. I want to help out – what can I do?" Melinda asked, looking at the deacon and his petite wife.

"You can help me here in the house. Don't worry about wearing Amish clothing. What you have packed should be fine, as long as it's modest," said Mrs. Mast.

Melinda nodded quickly. "Thank you. I'll be careful about what I wear."

Half an hour later, she was busy, kneading bread dough with her bare hands. Once that had been done, she peeled and chopped fresh vegetables for that night's supper – fried chicken, baked potatoes and vegetables. Smelling the delicious scents of the cooking food, she felt her stomach rumble.

After supper was over, Melinda helped with dishes and cleaning up the kitchen. Exhausted from the long, eventful day she'd just experienced, Melinda sat outside on the wide, deep back porch enjoying the sunshine.

By Saturday, Melinda was beginning to get used to the routine of the Mast house.

"We need to clean every room on the first floor, Melinda. You and my daughters will all do that – tomorrow's meeting takes place here, and everything must sparkle!" the older woman said as she handed Melinda a cloth and bucket.

By the end of that day, Melinda's hands, arm and back were one big mass of pain. Still, she pitched in to help with supper preparations.

The next morning, she woke up and chose a respectful blouse and skirt in shades of green. She was directed where to sit and, listening to the sing-song German cadences, she still felt peace entering her spirit. One of the Mast girls sat with her, telling her what was being said. Listening to everything, she realized why the Amish lived as they did. She thought about everything she'd heard and learned as she helped to take trays and bowls of food to the long tables for the community members' lunch. When it was her turn to sit down, she felt her eyes continually straying over to Steven. As she ate, she realized she was attracted to him.

Two Amish women asked if they could join her. Nodding, she said it was fine.

"Welcome to Hope Crossing, Miss Abbott," the younger one said with a friendly smile.

"Thank you. Why is lunch served the way it is? In shifts, I mean," Melinda asked trying not to stare at Steven.

"Because there are so many of us and not enough benches – or space to put them," the older woman said. "Therefore, we start with the oldest community members – out of respect – and clean up for everyone until the children are able to eat. The youngest children eat with their families, no matter their ages."

***

Melinda was learning how to make bread from scratch when the sheriff knocked at the Mast's front door. She answered, letting him in.

"How are you settling in?" he asked, removing his hat.

"I'm getting used to it – although each day brings new lessons and surprises," Melinda said escorting the sheriff to the kitchen.

"You might want to sit down, Miss Abbott. Mrs. Mast, where's your husband and son?" the sheriff asked as he stood wide-legged at the entrance to the kitchen.

"Steven is working and my husband is coming back from an errand," Mrs. Mast said as she wiped flour from her hands.

"What is it?"

"Mr. Scott has come back from Montana. My deputy was called to your condo because of a loud disturbance he caused. When he found you'd left, he got pretty mad, because he doesn't know where you are. We're going to continue providing 24-hour protection to Hope Crossing. If you see him, call me right away," said the sheriff, looking from Mrs. Mast to Melinda and back again. "You," he said, pointing at Melinda, "must stay here. I'm afraid that your boyfriend is dangerous."

"We will, right away, Sheriff. Thank you," said Mrs. Mast with her eyes wide.

Melinda, standing to her side, wanted to slide into a hole and disappear forever. She felt that, because of her work with Troy, she was responsible for the current situation.

"I am so sorry, Mrs. Mast! If it hadn't been for me..."

"Oh, hush, Melinda. Your part in this is over. You've repented and you are forgiven. You are in just as much danger as we are, and we will protect you. Hmmm?" Mrs. Mast fixed Melinda with a sharp, no-nonsense look.

"Thank you. I just keep thinking that, if I had been acting like a Christian, this wouldn't have happened." As soon as the words came out, Melinda was stunned.

"Anyway, ladies, I need to get my deputies deployed around Hope Crossing. You lock your doors and windows. Clear?"

"Ya. Thank you." Motioning to Melinda, Mrs. Mast saw the sheriff out the door and began bustling around, closing and locking doors and windows.

"Miss Abbott! Martha! Are you two all right?" shouted Deacon Mast when he came in.

"Yes, we are. Everything's locked up tight," Mrs. Mast said.

"I must meet with the school board. We have to decide what to do about the scholars," said the deacon. "I will be back by suppertime." Placing his hat back on his head, he strode outside and was gone.

***

The school board and teacher decided to temporarily suspend school sessions until Troy was captured.

"Scholars, you will work on your books and schoolwork at home, every day, until we can resume school. Every day, work on your subjects. Use the schedules I gave you after we came back from our Christmas break," said the young teacher. "Now, your parents are here. Go, and be safe!"

Scholars scattered, carrying their books, notebooks and lunch pails. Parents waited outside, not breathing easily until their children were safely in their buggies.

CHAPTER FOURTEEN

At the Mast home, Mrs. Mast asked Melinda to work with the children, helping them with their daily assignments. Melinda was excited and eager to take on the work – at least, now she was doing something! Something that mattered – as she worked with the children, she smiled as they caught onto a new concept. When lessons were over, the children were either put to work or allowed to play inside the large, spacious living room.

On one day when Melinda and Martha Mast were returning from the Amish market, Melinda gasped, seeing Troy's huge, blocky Hummer. Putting her hand on the other woman's forearm, she said, "Martha, look over there! That's Troy's car!"

Martha gasped and made the horse turn down a side road.

"You're in danger right now. The bishop lives in that house on the right side of the road. We're stopping here so we can keep you safe and call the sheriff," she said, pulling on the reins. She and Melinda jumped out of the buggy and hurried to the front porch.

Inside, Martha explained what was happening. The bishop's eyes widened and he ran outside to his barn to call the sheriff. Five minutes later, deputies pulled up and fanned out along the Hope Crossing roads. As fast as they had responded, they were unable to locate Troy.

Back at the Mast house, Mark Mast sat down with Melinda. Resting his elbows on his thighs he gazed solemnly at Melinda.

"You have to stay inside the house until they arrest your man friend, Melinda. I am sorry. It's for your own safety."

"Oh, no, deacon, don't worry! It's because of me..." Melinda started, breaking off when the deacon raised a work-worn hand.

"You have repented. Nonetheless, you must stay inside."

Melinda nodded silently. "Thank you for being so forgiving."

After supper that night, Melinda was sitting in the kitchen, thinking about a possible return to work when Steven sat down next to her with a writing pad and pencil in his hand.

"Miss Abbott... Melinda, can you explain Mr. Scott's habits and his plans to take our children, please? If you would, writing them down would help," he said, giving her a shy smile.

"Yes. If it'll help, I'll do anything!" said Melinda as she took the proffered pad and pencil. Thinking, she wrote down what she knew of Troy's recent schedule and plans to grab the children of the district. When she was done, she turned and gave her work back to Steven. Looking at him, she realized he was becoming friendlier toward her. She also realized that he couldn't stop looking at her.

I can't figure this man out. The Amish usually marry fairly young. He's my age and still single – he puts a wall up in between us and I don't think it's just shyness or dislike.

That night, in her room, Melinda couldn't stop thinking about Steven. She wanted to get to know him better, but until Troy was captured, she also knew she couldn't think of Steven in any context, let alone move ahead with him.

That same day, Rachel Troyer learned that she was also in increased danger.

"You cannot go to the Amish market to sell your baked goods, Rachel. Not until this man is caught and put in jail. Your *mamm* and I will take them to the market and sell them for you – you just keep making them and we will sell them," Abel said, looking at his daughter.

"But *daed*, your own work! What about it?" Rachel asked, looking at her parents in shock.

"Your safety is more important. You only go to market once a week. We will be fine selling your goods that one day a week. Besides, what you sell helps with our bills. We will be fine,"

Barbara Troyer said. "Your grandparents will stay here at the house while we are gone. You will not be alone."

Rachel nodded, feeling shivers of fear skating down her skin. As her skin chilled, she rubbed her hands up and down her arms.

That night, as Thomas visited, he told her, "I will be coming here every night, Rachel. Until that man is caught, I will be visiting you every evening." Thomas looked at Rachel, knowing that he needed to see her every day to assure himself that his beloved was safe.

***

The following week, Thomas and Rachel were visiting in the living room when Thomas angled his long body and looked at Rachel.

"Rachel, I have something to ask you. I want you to think seriously before you respond – I want to spend the rest of my life with you. Would you consider marrying me? I... love you," he said, with his face becoming bright red.

Rachel's smile lit up her face as she flapped her hands trying to stay calm.

"Yes! I don't need to think about it, Thomas! I will marry you! And... I love you, too," she said whispering the last four words.

Thomas grabbed one of her hands exhaling in relief.

"Good! We have several months before the next Wedding Season begins. Shall we tell your parents?"

The couple walked into the kitchen, where they told Abel and Barbara of their engagement and plans to marry that fall. Rachel found herself enveloped in hugs from both of her parents then Abel shook Thomas' hand. Later that night, after Rachel had gotten ready for bed, she opened the door to her *mamm's* light knock.

"We will need to plan on deciding what color you want your wedding dress to be. Then we need to make it, along with your new prayer *kapp* and apron," Barbara said.

"Ya! We'll be busy, *mamm*!"

"First, let's deal with this *Englischer* and let our lives get back to normal. Then, we can plan your wedding," said Barbara with a gentle smile at her youngest child.

The sheriff's department continued looking for Troy Scott. Using a drawing that Melinda had made, they were alert for every dark, large SUV that passed through Elkhart and Hope Crossing.

It was late one afternoon when Melinda pulled her head back into the house. She had noticed storm clouds building around and over Hope Crossing. Her heart stilled as she saw a dark, blocky SUV in the far distance. Focusing her vision a little more closely, she realized that Troy had snuck back into Hope Crossing. Gasping quickly she backed into the kitchen and closed the door. As she did she bumped into Steven.

"Steven, he's out there! Troy! He's on that side road going toward the school!" Melinda said, pointing in the direction of the road just west of the house.

"Stay here! *Denki!*" Steven pulled the door open and vaulted off the porch. Hitting the ground running, he angled straight for the barn, where he called the sheriff's office.

Again, despite the speed with which the deputies responded, they were unable to locate Troy's Hummer. Melinda was once again restricted to the indoors for her safety.

The following Monday, it was still fairly early when Melinda offered to hang out the freshly washed clothing.

"It's early. Troy's never up before 9 in the morning unless he's on a contract job," she told Martha. "I'll hang the clothes up and get straight inside. I promise."

"Okay, straight back inside. He's a danger to you, and you know that," Martha said handing her the large basket of clothing.

Melinda set the basket down and began pulling towels, sheets, pants, shirts and dresses out and hanging them on the clothesline. She was nearly done when she heard the distinctive sound of Troy's SUV door as it shut. With no hesitation, Melinda dropped the shirt she was holding and ran straight for the back door. Hearing the heavy pounding of Troy's steps behind her, she skimmed up the steps and into the back door barely in time.

"Troy... outside!"

"Let me get Steven. He came back in a minute ago..." Martha said. Running into the hallway she grabbed Steven who bolted out the front door. As he shut the door, Steven realized that several of their Amish neighbors had spotted Troy and followed him onto their land. Flying off the porch with a leap, he landed lightly in back of Troy, who was looking around wildly for an avenue of escape. The Amish men surrounded Troy, standing shoulder to shoulder, but not touching him.

Deacon Mast, Abel Troyer, John Schrock, Bishop Bontrager and Deacon Hershberger all stood around Troy.

"Mr. Scott, we don't want to hurt you. Just tell us why you want our children," the bishop asked.

Troy had become insane with his desire to expose the Amish as a cult. With this one thought in mind, he responded.

"You all are a dangerous cult. We... I have to stop you. Where's Melinda? She's been helping me. I need her help..."

Steven shivered at the tone in Troy's voice. Looking at his *daed* and the other men, he saw that they weren't moving – just standing around the *Englischer* man and keeping him from bolting.

"Mr. Scott, please sit in this chair while we wait," Deacon Mast said.

Troy sat looking wildly from man to man.

"Hey, we believe in allowing everyone to determine their own paths in life. That includes your kids – all kids, all adults, even. It's wrong, what y'all have been doing. Melinda was helping me. Where is she?"

"She's been helping us. She admitted to everything she did and she now realizes that we don't force our beliefs on anyone, let alone on our youth," the bishop said calmly.

Troy was stunned at what he heard. He couldn't believe Melinda had been turned!

Standing quickly he balled his fists, swung one and grinned with satisfaction as he connected with John Schrock's hard jaw. The older man grunted in shock and went down, then sat up quickly.

In response the five remaining men grabbed Troy and forced him to sit back down. Just then, the sheriff and one of his deputies arrived.

CHAPTER FIFTEEN

"Well, we finally caught up to him!" The sheriff smiled with satisfaction pulling his handcuffs from the back of his service belt, as he approached the small circle of men.

Troy was sitting on the chair and looking wildly around him. Seeing one of the Amish men turn to greet the sheriff and deputy, he seized his opportunity. He catapulted out of the chair and flew off the porch. Landing heavily with his arms wind-milling, he ran straight for his Hummer. Jamming the key into the ignition, he started his car and drove off going down one road after another. The sheriff and deputy ran to their cars and gave chase pursuing Troy, sirens blaring.

Troy aimed his Hummer toward the Amish school house. As he got closer to the school, he let out a cackle – he had spotted an Amish teen walking home from his father's barn to the house. Troy angled his vehicle so that he could open the door and trap the boy. Jumping out he grabbed the boy's arms and forced him into the SUV then putting the vehicle into gear, he took off once again.

Both lawmen saw Troy force the youngster into his vehicle. Gunning their vehicles, they got nearer to him, following Troy as he drove towards the empty school house.

Troy jumped out of the vehicle, hauling the frightened boy out with him by one arm. He ran from window to window looking for signs of students inside.

"Where are they? School's supposed to be in session! Where are the kids?" Troy yelled at the boy, but before the frightened boy could answer, Troy pushed him to the ground standing right over him and continuing to yell at him. "Tell me where they are! I have to rescue them! TELL ME!"

The boy, looking up at the tall, out-of-control *Englischer*, continued to cower on the ground. He was small, thin and barely an adolescent. He had been warned about the crazy *Englischers* stalking children, but it was different when one grabbed you in reality. He was crying, trying to figure a way out of this mess. "Sir, we're out of school. Studying at home. Until they capture... you! You're the *Englischer* that's been trying to take us!"

Lying on his back he scooted backwards as he saw Troy bend down to try and grab him again. His name was Jacob, but most people called him Scooter because he could move so fast. He was thin, lithe and all muscle from working on the farm. At only twelve years old, he could outrun some boys 18 years of age. He got to his feet, backing away from the crazed

Englischer. He turned and started running towards the corn field. It was nigh on spring and the corn was sprouting up; Jacob knew if he made it to the fields, he could escape this crazy man and get back home. He ran and Troy, forgetting the pursuing police vehicles, ran after him. "I'm trying to save you!" he screamed.

"I don't need to be saved except from you!" Jacob shouted over his shoulder as he ran. His brown hair normally fell at his shoulders now blew in the breeze his running was making. He didn't slow down or look back; he just kept going into the cornfield and away from the *Englischer*.

"Freeze, Scott! Let that boy go, right now!" The sheriff shouted in a commanding and penetrating voice as he leaped from his car withdrawing his weapon.

Jacob looked back; seeing the sheriff he slowed and then stopped running. Troy, seeing that the boy had slowed, started walking towards him. "I just want to save you."

Jacob backed away from the stranger. The sheriff's deputy ran towards Troy then launched himself much like a high school football player tackling a quarterback, making contact with Troy's back and sending Troy sprawling.

When Troy tried to get up, he was forced back down onto the fragrant lawn as the deputy landed right on top of him. Troy struggled, trying to get out from under the heavy, muscular deputy.

"Agh! Let me go! I have a mission to complete!" Troy felt first one arm, then the other, yanked behind his back as the deputy sat on him and locked the handcuffs on him. Both the deputy and sheriff grabbed Troy's arms and pulled him upright.

"Go with me to take him to the hospital's mental health ward. What we both heard probably warrants a stay for a few days." The sheriff put Troy into the back of the sheriff's car, and locked the seatbelt around him, locked the car doors and drove him to the hospital in Elkhart, where he was involuntarily committed for a five-day mental health evaluation.

***

As word spread through Hope Crossing, families began to relax, knowing that the danger to their community had been removed. Families were able to allow their children outside to help with outdoor and household chores; the children could play in safety outside once again.

The school board decided to resume school so scholars could finish out the year and take their examinations. Bishop Bontrager decided it was safe, once again, for district families to resume bi-weekly meetings. Looking at the schedule he had written, he notified the Hershberger family that they would be hosting the next meeting, scheduled two weeks later.

Melinda Abbott returned to her condo in Elkhart. Knowing that Troy would not be discharged from the mental health hospital, she felt safe in returning home. Unlocking the door and opening windows so she could air the stale rooms out, she unpacked and put her belongings away. As she did, she puzzled over what had happened in the Mast home.

"Miss Abbott... Melinda... I know you're going home today," Steven had said, approaching her outside. "I know you aren't Amish, but for some reason, I find myself drawn to you... I would like to get to know you better."

Melinda had looked at the handsome man in shock. "But... I thought y'all couldn't... uh..." Melinda, normally able to express herself, blushed as she found she was stumbling over her words.

"Get to know *Englischers*?" Steven grinned shyly, his dark-brown eyes sparkling. "It's not very common, no. But it isn't expressly forbidden, either. Here in Hope Crossing, Bishop Bontrager and the deacons all know that our community is so small that we need to be open to the possibility." Here, Steven became very serious. "I... I courted an Amish girl several years ago. We were engaged to be married. She was killed three months before we were supposed to be married. She had been coming home from delivering a quilt to her *Englischer* customer when a drunk driver hit and killed her. Ever since then, I haven't..."

"Been interested or wanted to meet anyone?" Melinda said softly. So that was what was in his past! Melinda's heart squeezed painfully as she realized the pain he must have been through.

"No. And... there aren't very many Amish women in our community who are over twenty-one, who are still single either," he said.

"Oh." Melinda still didn't know what to say.

"If you do not want to..." Steven said, getting up suddenly

"No! Oh, no! You just took me by surprise, that's all." Melinda gestured at the comfortable rocker. "Please, let's talk. Because... well, because I am interested. I find myself drawn to your faith – and you," she said softly, blushing.

Steven also blushed as he smiled in relief.

"Good. I know you're going back to your home in Elkhart. We need to talk about why we are interested in each other as well as in what makes us so different to each other. I need to warn you – we have some strong traditionalists here in Hope Crossing who will object to any... relationship we might have. Also, I want you to know that I'm interested in more than a casual relationship. I wasn't happy when you first moved in... but as I got to know you, I felt your reaching out for more knowledge. You... do want to learn more about our faith... right?"

Melinda nodded. "I do. Something about your beliefs draws me in. I feel... a peace I've never felt before when I listen to the prayers, sermons and hymns. If I had known I would feel this when... well, when Troy and I first started trying to come here and get to talk to you, I would never have decided to call y'all a cult or take your kids."

"I think God wanted you to meet us... maybe it would have been better if that meeting hadn't come with..." Steven struggled to find the right word.

"Misconceptions? Assumptions? Because that's what they were. I really thought that you controlled your kids too much, then when I listed to Rachel Troyer's interview again, I realized we – I – was wrong. I tried to convince Troy of that, but he refused to listen," Melinda said sadly.

"About... Mr. Scott... do you still have feelings for him?" Steven asked. His eyes were wide as he gazed at Melinda.

"Oh, no! When I realized that he wasn't going to let go of our thoughts that you were a cult... and when he yelled at me, I realized that was the end of our relationship. I don't take easily to being mistreated. Then, when it became clear that he had developed an obsession, I knew he would be a danger to me, as well as to everyone here in Hope Crossing. My plan..." Melinda tried not to sob. "My plan had been for us to be in a committed relationship. But..."

"It wasn't meant to be. That's all. You shouldn't make your decision right now. Instead, think and pray about it, in the stillness of your home. See where God leads you. If it is meant to be, it will happen," Steven said, softly.

Melinda nodded and gave him a shaky smile. He and his

father drove her to Elkhart and stayed as her vehicle was taken out of storage. Because it had been parked for so long, the battery needed to be jump-started. Once it had been running for a while, Mark Mast put her luggage in the back and shook her hand.

Steven took her hand and held onto it for several seconds. "Remember. Pray. See what God tells you in the stillness of your heart," he said.

Melinda came back to the present in her well-appointed condo. Looking around, she realized the differences between her home and the Amish homes. Getting a chilled bottle of water from the refrigerator, she twisted the lid off and took a long swallow as she sat down.

She thought about her weeks living in Hope Crossing and getting to know the district's members. Rachel Troyer and her easy smile and trust... Mary Schrock, her spirit and love of her lifestyle. Mark and Martha Mast. Thomas Schrock. Barbara and John Schrock. The bishop and his deacons. Steven. They didn't have to forgive her and welcome her into their community as they had. Melinda marveled at their ability to forgive and let history stay in the past. She thought about how willing they had been to put themselves in danger, housing her, just to keep her safe.

God, that is the essence – no, not even the essence – the demonstration of love! I only hope that I can forgive myself in time. Melinda shifted restlessly on the sofa as she thought.

She thought of her new friends. Rachel and Mary were now able to return to selling their baked goods at the Amish market, not having to rely on their parents to sell them.

I'm just grateful that Troy is put away so that he won't put them in danger any more. Those children get the opportunity to explore life away from Hope Crossing. Their parents allow them to experiment – something I didn't realize until it was nearly too late. When the children come back, they make the decision to come back – they aren't forced to do so. I . . . we didn't know that, either. Rachel, I'm glad I listened to your interview again. And I thank God that I was able to listen and hear with an open mind.

Melinda turned her television on and went into the kitchen to make a quick dinner. As she ate the frozen meal she had put into the microwave, she pulled a face. The taste she used to like now tasted... nasty. Throwing the food away, she drove to the store and picked up the makings for a fresh salad. While she was in the store, she bought chicken, fish and other foods so she could cook her meals from scratch. Back at home, she made a fast salad and ate as she continued to think about all the changes she had been through.

I wonder. I know the Amish don't accept computers because they are a convenience that could make me feel too much pride. But I need to continue my work. If I start getting to know Steven better – this sounds weird, but if he begins to court me – it might be with the expectation that a relationship – any relationship – would be long-term.

After eating, Melinda did some research and found that non-Amish who were courted by someone in the Amish faith could potentially keep their computers as long as they were used only for work purposes.

Okay, gal, don't go running down that road yet. Steven told you to think and pray, not plan a wedding. That thought caused Melinda to jump convulsively. *Oh! If... if God wants it to go that way, I would be expected to be baptized into the Amish faith. That much I know. I would also have to start wearing the same kind of clothes the women wear – the dresses,* kapps *and aprons.*

Melinda continued to think about this as she sat sideways on her armchair. Her thoughts wandered to the differences between the unmarried and married Amish men. The married men grew beards after marriage, no longer shaving. Settling down in her armchair, Melinda began to daydream about the strong and handsome Steven – seeing him clean-shaven, she began to imagine him with a long, brown beard.

Next, Melinda's thoughts took her to his recounting of how his fiancée had been killed. They were probably in their early 20's. I'm twenty-five and I think he's about the same age. Oh, God, he's been alone and grieving for that long!

EPILOGUE

Now that Troy Scott had been caught, Hope Crossing residents were able to move about freely once again. Parents allowed their children to go to their friends' houses and roam around the area when their chores were completed.

Rachel rejoiced as she baked the next day's goods for the Amish market.

"How much do you have available to take to market?" Barbara asked as she entered the kitchen.

"Quite a bit. Cookies, cakes, brownies and pies," Rachel replied. "I'm just grateful that I can start selling them again, instead of having to rely on you and *Daed*. Now, he can work."

"*Nee*, it was no problem, Rachel. The problem was that *Englischer* losing his mind, and thinking he had the right to kidnap our children and threaten you and Mary," Barbara stated with a shake of her head as she began working on supper.

"*Mamm*, how do you feel about Miss Abbott? Melinda?" Rachel asked curiously.

"Well. At first, I wasn't sure about the wisdom of bringing her here for her safety. But it became clear pretty fast that she had repented and wanted only our safety. Why do you ask?" Barbara asked as she began cooking the stew meat.

Rachel smiled with mischief. "Because... Steven Mast likes her." Rachel sobered fast. "And you know how long it has been since he lost Hannah in that accident."

"Well! They will have a hard journey as they get to know each other. Melinda will need to be baptized – if they decide to think of marriage. Not everyone here will be happy that Steven is looking beyond Hope Crossing for a wife," Barbara said, adding chopped onion to the sautéed meat.

"*Nee*, but, *Mamm*. There are no women close to his age that he can court. Besides, I've been watching and getting to know Melinda and I think she is sincere about her desire to learn about our faith. She and I talked after the last meeting and she really wanted to know about why we do things the way we do. It was... more than her reporter's curiosity, *Mamm*. She really wanted to know so she could fill herself with knowledge. Honestly, I think that, if Steven and Melinda decide to court, he will find a good future wife," Rachel said, looking at Barbara.

"Oh, ho, ho! 'Future wife,' huh? Well. Let's see what happens. I hope Steven told her to think and pray before making a decision. That way, we – and he – will know that their decision is one that has been guided by God," Barbara said, nodding her head.

"Steven is a devout, God-loving man, *Mamm*. I'm sure he has asked her to think and pray before making any decision about courting. *Mamm*, let's pray for them and help them get to know each other," Rachel pleaded.

And so they did.

The End.

THANK YOU FOR READING!

And thank you for supporting me as an independent author. I hope you enjoyed reading this as much as I loved writing it! I hope you enjoyed reading this as much as I enjoyed writing it! If so, you can read a sample of the next book in the next chapter.

Lastly, if you enjoyed this book and want to continue to support my writing, please leave me a review to let everyone know what you thought of my work. It's the best thing you can do to keep indie authors like me writing. (And if you find something in the book that – YIKES – makes you think it deserves less than 5-stars, drop me a line at Rachel.stoltzfus@globagrafxpress.com, and I'll fix it if I can)

All the best,

Rachel

NEIGHBORING FAITHS

AN AMISH COUNTRY QUARREL 3

Is love enough for Melinda Abbott to turn her back on her Englisch life and career? And if so, will the Amish community she attempted to harm ever accept her?

After Melinda Abbott repents for her ill-advised attempt to rescue the children of Hope Crossing from a non-existent cult, she finds herself growing closer to the people she once planned to harm. In spite of herself, Melinda is drawn to the Plain lifestyle and the connections she has made in the Amish community. Especially Steven Mast, a young Amish man who just might capture her heart. But is love enough for Melinda to turn her back on her Englisch life and career? And even if she wants to be a part of Hope Crossing, is the community ready to accept her?

CHAPTER ONE

Melinda

Driving back from Hope Crossing, Melinda's fingers tapped on the steering wheel as she listened to an upbeat jazz tune. She felt... positive about a potential courting relationship with Steven Mast, now that she'd had some time to think about their attraction to each other. She was still unsure though if she would be able to handle life as an Amish woman. She had enjoyed her day in the Mast home, and the conversation she'd had with his mother about following the Amish belief system, but it was one thing to discuss something and another thing to live it.

If this attraction she felt for Steven did grow into something more, would that be enough to bridge the differences between them?

Certainly, the Amish were nothing like the group that had gotten hold of Jim.

Brainwashed him...

Melinda, not wanting to become depressed over her cousin's involvement with a true cult, drew in a deep breath and reminded herself that the Amish refused to evangelize for a good reason.

Once at home, she brought in the baked goods she and Martha had made while she was there for the day. Realizing the heat of the day had made her condo hot, she closed the blinds and turned up the air conditioning.

Standing in front of the vent as it kicked a cool blast of air into her face, Melinda again wondered what she was thinking with this courtship with Steven. She wouldn't have air conditioning, or a microwave, or any of the dozens of comforts she now took for granted if she joined the Amish.

Would she even be able to do her work?

Maybe she should just tell Steven to forget the courtship. The last thing she wanted was to lead him on.

But still, something kept Steven and her conversation with his mother in Melinda's heart.

She had always said that if she did find love that she would hold onto it. Keep it sacred.

Steven, and the Amish, deserved a chance. Wasn't that what a courtship was, like dating, a chance to get to know each other better and see how you might fit together?

In spur of the moment action, Melinda switched off the air-conditioning, walked to the windows of her apartment, and opened them wide. A hot, sluggish breeze wafted in through the blinds.

Then she showered, keeping the water just to the side of chilly, and wearing her towel, made dinner.

She could read tonight instead of watching the television.

Maybe if she started taking little steps now, she would get comfortable enough without her comforts to transition to an Amish lifestyle.

If this was love, after all.

Rachel

Rachel Troyer read her Bible that evening and thought about Melinda Abbott. While the *Englischer* woman's early actions had threatened the youth of their community, Rachel had seen a change for the positive in Melinda – she wanted to learn about the Amish, not only to satisfy her curiosity, but because something about their lifestyle and faith called to her.

Lord, if it is your will, make it possible for her to become a part of our Hope Crossing community. I sense something... sad in her past, and your love could help her heal. I have seen Martha Mast warming to her as well and there is something growing between Melinda and Steven Mast. Lord, I know that it is very unusual for non-Amish to become a member of an Amish family, but if it will benefit both Melinda and Hope Crossing, I would like to see her and Steven Mast begin courting.

Steven

Steven sat outside on his porch as the sun painted gold and red over his fields and thought about Melinda. He remembered his initial resistance to having her move into his parents' home, then, as they got to know her, realized he was beginning to like what he was getting to know.

She was truly repentant of what she had begun to try to do to Hope Crossing. When she realized just how dangerous Troy Scott was, she helped the bishop and church leadership to catch him whenever he came to our district. I felt her becoming more peaceful and I don't know, settled, the longer she lived with us. That she is at least considering our courting tells me that she wants more than just a superficial relationship with us here at Hope Crossing.

***

Morning dawned with a dazzling sun that cascaded across the fields, increasing heat and the trill of saccades foretelling more warmth as time passed. Barbara and her daughter, Rachel rattled along gently in their buggy, headed toward an *Englischer* fabric store in Elkhart. They were in search of fabric for Rachel's wedding dress, prayer *kapp* and apron.

"*Mamm*, now that we're here, can we try to find out where Melinda lives?"

"Don't we have her business card?"

"I wasn't thinking." Rachel shrugged sheepishly. "I left it at home in the kitchen. But I would like to know so I can visit Melinda in the future, and we're here now. I also want to invite her to our house so she can start learning about our lifestyle," Rachel smiled, a broad smile that traveled from her lips up to her sparkly hazel eyes.

"That is an excellent idea, daughter! Maybe we can ask to look through the phone book at the fabric store and we can find her that way."

"That might work – I hope it will, anyway! Oh, it is so hot today!" Rachel fanned herself with both hands.

"*Ya*, it is. Would you like to stop to buy something cold to drink? A lemonade or an iced tea, perhaps?" her mother suggested, pulling into the fabric store's parking lot.

"*Ya*! I'll pay," Rachel offered. Inside the store, they browsed through the store's large selection of plain fabrics, ultimately deciding on a sky-blue fabric which Rachel could wear to Sunday meeting services for the next several years. Taking the fabric bolts to the counter, her mother ordered what they would need and then paid for it.

"Oh! Before I forget, do you have a telephone book we could borrow? We need to find a local number," she said, remembering as she took the large bag of fabric.

"Here you go, ma'am," the clerk returned with a thin yellow and white book.

Five minutes later, Rachel and Barbara looked at each other in confusion. Melinda's name didn't show up in the directory.

"Is there something I can help you with?" the manager asked...

THANK YOU FOR READING!

And thank you for supporting me as an independent author. I hope you enjoyed reading this as much as I loved writing it!

If so, look for this book in eBook or Paperback format at your favorite online book distributors. Also, when a series is complete, we usually put out a discounted collection. If you'd rather read the entire series at once and save a few bucks doing it, we recommend looking for the collection.

Lastly, if you enjoyed this book and want to continue to support my writing, please leave me a review to let everyone know what you thought of my work. It's the best thing you can do to keep indie authors like me writing. (And if you find something in the book that – YIKES – makes you think it deserves less than 5-stars, drop me a line at Rachel.stoltzfus@globagrafxpress.com, and I'll fix it if I can)

All the best,

Rachel

ABOUT THE AUTHOR

Rachel was born and raised in Lancaster, Pennsylvania. Being a neighbor of the Mennonite community, she started writing Amish romance fiction as a way of looking at the Amish community. She wanted to present a fair and honest representation of a love that is both romantic and sweet. She hopes her readers enjoy her efforts.

Made in the USA
Middletown, DE
11 September 2019